Catherine Owen

Choice Cookery

Catherine Owen

Choice Cookery

ISBN/EAN: 9783744767477

Printed in Europe, USA, Canada, Australia, Japan

Cover: Foto ©Andreas Hilbeck / pixelio.de

More available books at **www.hansebooks.com**

CHOICE COOKERY

BY

CATHERINE OWEN

AUTHOR OF

"TEN DOLLARS ENOUGH" "GENTLE BREAD-WINNERS" ETC.

NEW YORK

HARPER & BROTHERS, FRANKLIN SQUARE

1889

PREFACE.

CHOICE cookery is not intended for households that have to study economy, except where economy is a relative term; where, perhaps, the housekeeper could easily spend a dollar for the materials of a luxury, but could not spare the four or five dollars a caterer would charge.

Many families enjoy giving little dinners, or otherwise exercising hospitality, but are debarred from doing so by the fact that anything beyond the ordinary daily fare has to be ordered in, or an expensive extra cook engaged. And although we may regret that hospitality should ever be dependent on fine cooking, we have to take things as they are. It is not every hostess who loves simplicity that dares to practise it.

It was to help the women who wish to know at a glance what is newest and best in modern cookery that these chapters were written for *Harper's Bazar*, and are now gathered into a book. It is hoped by the writer that the copious details and simplification of different matters will enable those who have already achieved success in the plainer branches of cookery to venture further, and realize for themselves that it is only the "first step that costs."

I have to acknowledge my indebtedness to Mrs. Clarke, of the South Kensington School of Cookery, to Madame de Salis, and those epicurean friends who have cast their nets in foreign waters, and sent me the daintiest fish they caught.

CONTENTS.

CHOICE COOKERY.

I.

INTRODUCTION.

By choice cookery is meant exactly what the words imply. There will be no attempt to teach family or inexpensive cooking, those branches of domestic economy having been so excellently treated by capable hands already. It may be said *en passant*, however, that even choice cooking is not necessarily expensive. Many dishes cost little for the materials, but owe their daintiness and expensiveness to the care bestowed in cooking or to a fine sauce. For instance: cod, one of the cheapest of fish, and considered coarse food as usually served, becomes an

1

epicurean dish when served with a fine Hollandaise or oyster sauce, and it will not even then be more expensive than any average-priced boiling fish. Flounder served as *sole Normande* conjures up memories of the famous Philippe, whose fortune it made, or it may be of luxurious little dinners at other famous restaurants, and is suggestive, in fact, of anything but economy. Yet it is really an inexpensive dish.

But while it is quite true that fine cooking does not always mean expensive cooking, it is also true that it requires the best materials and sufficient of them; that if satisfactory results are to be obtained there must be no attempt to stint or change proportions from a false idea of economy, although it must never be forgotten that all good cooking is economical, by which I mean that there is no waste, every cent's worth of material being made to do its full duty.

In this book the object will be to give the newest and most *recherché* dishes, and these will naturally be expensive. Yet for those families who depend upon the caterer for everything in the way of fine soups, *entrées*, or sauces, because the cook can achieve only the plain part of the dinner, it will be found a great economy as well as convenience to be independent of this outside resource, which is always very costly, and invariably destroys the individuality of a repast. Many new recipes will be given, and others little known in private kitchens, or thought to be quite beyond the attainment of any but an accomplished *chef*. But if strict attention be paid to small matters, and the directions faithfully carried out, there will be no difficulty in a lady becoming her own *chef*.

I propose to begin with sauces. This is reversing the usual mode, and yet I think the reader will not regret the innovation. The cooking to be taught in these pages, being emphatically what is popularly known as " Delmonico cooking," very much depends on the excellence of the sauces served with each dish; and as it is no time to learn to make a fine sauce when the dish it is served with is being cooked, I think the better plan is to give the sauces first. They will be frequently referred to, but no repetition of the recipes will be given.

Before proceeding further I will say a few words that may save time and patience hereafter. Of course it is not expected that any one will hope to succeed with elaborate dishes without understanding the principles of simple cooking, but many do this without perceiving that in that knowledge they hold the key to very much more, and I would ask readers who are in earnest about the matter to acquire the habit of putting two and two together in cooking as they would in fancy-work. If you know half a dozen embroidery or lace stitches, you see at once that you can produce the elaborate combinations in which those stitches are used. So it is with cooking. The most elaborate dish will only be a combination of two or three simpler processes of cooking, *perfectly* done—that is a *sine qua non*—something fried, roasted, boiled, or braised to perfection, and a sauce that no *chef* could improve upon; but to recognize that this is so—that when you can make a Châteaubriand sauce or a Béarnaise perfectly, and can *sauté* a steak, the famed filets à la Châteaubriand or à la Béarnaise are no longer a mystery, or that one who can make clear meat jelly and roast a chicken has learned all but the arrangement of a *chaudfroid* in aspic—will make apparently complicated dishes simple.

I go into these matters because I hope to cause my readers to *think* about the recipes they will use, when they will see for themselves that even the finest cooking is not intricate nor in any way difficult. It requires intelligence and great care about details: no half-attention will do, any more than it will in any other thing we attempt, whether it be high art or domestic art.

In making sauces or reading recipes for

them it simplifies matters to remember that in savory sauces—by which I mean those served with meats or fish—there are what the .French call the two "mother sauces," white sauce and brown ; all others, with few exceptions, are modifications of these two ; that is to say, béchamel is only white sauce made with white stock and cream instead of milk ; allemande is the same, only yolks of eggs replace the cream ; and so on through the long list of sauces belonging to the blond variety. The simple brown sauce becomes the famous Châteaubriand by the addition of glaze (or very strong gravy) and a glass of white wine, and is the "mother" of many others equally fine. This being so, it will be seen that it is of the first importance that the making of these two "mother sauces" should be thoroughly understood, in order for the finer ones based on them to be successfully accomplished.

It will clear the way for easy work if I here give the directions for making one of the most necessary and convenient aids to fine cooking—the above-named glaze. To have it in the house saves much worry and work. If the soup is not just so strong as we wish, the addition of a small piece of glaze will make it excellent; or we wish to make brown sauce, and have no stock, the glaze comes to our aid. To have stock in the house at all times is by no means easy in a small family, especially in summer; with glaze, which is solidified stock, one is independent of it.

Six pounds of lean beef from the leg, or a knuckle of veal and beef to make six pounds. Cut this in pieces two inches square or less; do the same with half a pound of lean ham, free from rind or smoky outside, and which has been scalded five minutes. Put the meat into a two-gallon pot with three medium-sized onions with two cloves in each, a turnip, a carrot, and a *small* head of celery. Pour over them five quarts of cold water; let it come slowly to the boiling-point, when skim,

and draw to a spot where it will gently simmer for six hours. This stock as it is will
be an excellent foundation for all kinds of
clear soups or gravies, with the addition of
salt, which must on no account be added for
glaze.

To reduce this stock to glaze, do as follows:
Strain the stock first through a colander, and
return meat and vegetables to the pot; put
to them four quarts of *hot* water, and let it
boil four hours longer. The importance of
this second boiling, which may at first sight
appear useless economy, will be seen if you
let the two stocks get cold; the first will
be of delightful flavor, but probably quite
liquid; the last will be flavorless, but if the
boiling process has been slow enough it will
be a jelly, the second boiling having been
necessary to extract the gelatine from the
bones, which is indispensable for the forma-
tion of glaze.

Strain both these stocks through a scalded
cloth. (If they have been allowed to get

cool, heat them in order to strain.) Put both stocks together into one large pot, and let it boil as fast as possible with the cover off, leaving a large spoon in it to prevent it boiling over, also to stir occasionally; when it is reduced to three pints put it into a small saucepan, and let it boil more slowly. Stir frequently with a wooden spoon until it begins to thicken and has a fine yellowish-brown color, which will be when it is reduced to a quart or rather less. At this point watch closely, as it quickly burns. When there is only a pint and a half it will be fit to pour into small cups or jars, or it may be dried in thin sheets, if required for soup in travelling; to do this, pour it into oiled tin pans an inch deep. When cold it can be cut out in two-inch squares and dried by exposure to the air till it is like glue. One square makes a cup of strong soup if dissolved in boiling water and seasoned. If, however, it is put into pots, it must *not be covered* until all moisture has evaporated and the glaze shrinks from the sides of the jar. This may take a month.

The most convenient of all ways for preserving glaze is to get from your butcher a yard of sausage-skin. Tie one end very tightly, then pour in the glaze while warm by means of a large funnel. Tie the skin just as you would sausage as close to the glaze as possible, cut off any remaining skin, and hang the one containing the glaze up to dry. When needed, a slice is cut from this.

Of course any strong meat and bone-soup can be boiled down in the same way, and where there is meat on hand in danger of spoiling from sudden change of weather it can be turned into glaze, and kept indefinitely. I have found glaze five years old as good as the first week.

II.

In addition to the glaze, for which the recipe is given in the preceding pages, and which will make you independent of the stock pot, there are several other articles involving very small outlay which it is absolutely necessary to have at hand in order to follow directions without trouble and worry.

It is often said by thoughtless housekeepers that cooking-books are of little use, because the recipes always call for something that is not in the house. This is a habit of mind only, for the very women who say it keep their work-baskets supplied with everything necessary for work, not only the every-day white and black spools, nor would they hesitate to undertake a piece of embroidery which required quite unusual combinations

of color or material, and to be obtained only
with difficulty. Grant a little of this earnest
painstaking to the requirements of the cook-
ing-book at the start, see that the herb-bot-
tles are supplied with dried herbs (when fresh
are not attainable), the spice-boxes contain
the small quantity of fresh fine spices that
is sufficient for a good deal of cooking, and
red and white wine and brandy are in the
house, all of which should be kept in the
store-closet for cooking alone, and not liable
to be " out " when wanted.

The so-called " French herbs " are rarely
found in American gardens, yet might be
very readily sown in early spring, as parsley
is ; but although seldom home-grown, they
are to be found at the French market-gar-
dener's in Washington Market, and can be
bought fresh and dried in paper bags quickly
for use. I say dried quickly, because unless
the sun is very hot much of the aroma will
pass into the air; it is, therefore, better to
dry them in a cool oven. When they are

dry enough to crumble to dust, free the herbs from stems and twigs, and put them separately into tin boxes or wide-mouthed bottles, each labelled. The expense of herbs and spices is very slight, and they are certainly not neglected among kitchen stores on that account; it is merely the want of habit in ordering them. In addition to these articles a bottle of capers, one of olives, one of anchovies, canned mushrooms, and canned truffles should be on hand—the latter should be bought in the smallest-sized cans, as they are very costly, but a little goes a long way. Families living in the country often have for a season more mushrooms than they can use. In the few days in which they are plentiful opportunity should be taken to peel and dry as many as possible; when powdered they give a finer flavor than the canned mushroom, and may be used to great advantage in dark sauces.

The French *chef* classes all white sauces as *blonde*, and calls the jar of very smooth thick

white sauce, which he keeps ready made as a
foundation for most of the family of light
sauces, his *blonde* or *velouté*. This explanation is given because directions are often
found in French recipes to "take half a pint
of velouté" or of "blonde." The mistress
of a private house may not find it wise or
necessary to keep a supply of sauce ready
made, although to one who has to supply a
variety of sauces each day it is indispensable;
but the day before a dinner-party sauces can
be so made, and covered with a film of butter to prevent skin forming, and can then
be heated in a bain-marie when required for
use. Almost every *chef* has his favorite
recipe for velouté, or white sauce, but they
differ only in points that are little essential;
the foundation is always the same, as follows: Put two ounces of butter in a thick
saucepan with two ounces of flour (tablespoonfuls approximate the ounce, but weight
only should be relied on for fine cooking).
Let these melt over the fire, stirring them

so that the butter and flour become well mixed; then let them bubble together, stirring enough to prevent the flour sticking or changing color. Three minutes will suffice to cook the flour; add a pint of clear hot white stock that has been strained through a cloth. This stock must not be poured slowly, or the sauce will thicken too fast. Hold the pint-measure or other vessel in which the stock may be in the left hand, stir the butter and flour quickly with the right, then turn the broth to it *all at once.* Let this simmer an hour until very thick, then add a gill of very rich cream, stir, and the sauce is ready.

This is undoubtedly the best way to make white sauce, which is to serve as a foundation for others, or is intended to mask meat or poultry, the long, slow simmering producing an extreme blandness not to be attained by a quicker method. But circumstances sometimes prevent the previous preparation of the sauce, in which case it may be made exactly in the same way, only instead of a pint of broth, but three gills should be poured on the butter and flour, and a gill of thick cream stirred in when it boils; the sauce is finished when it again reaches the boiling-point.

This is the foundation for the following "grand" sauces: Poulette, Allemande, Uxelles, Soubise, Ste. Ménehould, Périgueux, Suprême, besides all the simpler ones, which take their name from the chief ingredient, such as caper, cauliflower, celery, lobster, etc., etc.

For sauces that have vinegar or lemon juice, it is better that the velouté, or white sauce, should have no cream until the last minute, or it may curdle. My object in giving the recipes for sauces in the way I intend —that is to say, by building on to, or omitting from, one foundation sauce—is to dispel some of the confusion which exists in the minds of many people about the exact difference between several sauces differing from each other very slightly—a confusion which is only added to by reading over the fully written recipes for each, as many a painstaking, intelligent woman's headache will testify. As we progress, the exact difference between each will be explained.

Béchamel. — This sauce differs from the white sauce only in the fact that the white stock used for the latter need not be very strong; for béchamel it should either be very strong or boiled down rapidly to make it so, and there should always be half cream instead of one third, as in white sauce, and when required for fish the stock may be of fish. White sauce is frequently (perhaps most frequently) made with milk, or milk and cream, in place of stock, in this country, and answers admirably for many purposes, but would not be what is required for the kind of cooking intended in these pages.

Most readers know how "to stir," and it may seem quite an unnecessary matter to go into. Yet if only one reader does not know

2

that to stir means a regular, even, slow cir-
cling of the spoon, *not only in the centre* of
the saucepan, but round the sides, she will
fail in making good sauce.   Stir, then, slowly, gently, going over every part of the bottom of the saucepan till the sides are reached,
pass the spoon gently round them, thence
back to the middle, and so on.   In this way
the sauce gets no chance to stick to any particular spot.   A small copper saucepan is the
best possible utensil for making sauce, as it
does not burn.

The rule for seasoning is a level salt-spoonful of salt to half a pint; pepper, one fourth
the quantity.   This, however, is only when
the stock is unseasoned; if seasoned, only
salt enough must be added to season the
cream and eggs.

Allemande.—Take half a pint of white
sauce, add to it half the liquor from a can of
mushrooms, and half a dozen of the mushrooms chopped fine.   Let them simmer—
stirring all the time—five minutes, then re-

move from the fire. Set the saucepan into another containing boiling water. Have the yolks of three eggs ready beaten, put a little of the sauce to them, beat together, then add the eggs gradually to the rest of the sauce, which must be returned to the fire, and stirred until the eggs *begin* to thicken; then it must be quickly removed, and stirred until slightly cool. Season with a saltspoonful of salt, a fourth of one of pepper, and strain carefully.

It must never be forgotten that in thickening with eggs the sauce or soup must *not boil* after they are added, or they will curdle. Yet if they do not reach the boiling-point they will not thicken. Only keen attention to the first sign of thickening will insure success. If a failure is made the first time, look upon it as the first step to success, for you have learned what the danger *looks like*. Make the sauce again as soon as possible, so that your eye may not lose the impression. It is worth considerable effort (and it is really only a matter of a few minutes each time) to make Allemande sauce well, for in doing so you also learn to make Hollandaise and several choice sauces, as will be seen by those that follow.

Poulette Sauce. — Make Allemande sauce as directed in the foregoing recipe; add a wineglass of white wine. If sweetbreads or chicken are to be cooked in the sauce, as is not unusual, of course the eggs must be left out until the last thing. Anything served with this sauce is called *à la poulette.*

Sauce à la d' Uxelles. — Chop fine a dozen *small* button mushrooms, or half a dozen large ones; parsley and chives, of each enough to make a teaspoonful when finely chopped; of lean ham a tablespoonful, and one small shallot. Fry gently in a tablespoonful of butter, but do not let them brown. Stir these into half a pint of white sauce, simmer three or four minutes, then add two yolks of eggs, as for Allemande, and the last thing a half-teaspoonful of lemon-juice, and just enough glaze to make the sauce the shade of a pale Suède glove. This sauce is used cold to coat meats that have to be cooked in paper, and many that are afterwards to be fried in bread-crumbs, for which directions will be given in the *entrées.* Dishes termed *à la d' Uxelles* arc among the most *recherché* productions of the French kitchen.

Villeroi Sauce.—Make half a pint of white sauce, which, as in the case of béchamel, may be made of fish stock when for use with fish; chop half a dozen mushrooms, and add a gill of the liquor to the sauce, half a saltspoonful of powdered thyme (or one sprig, if fresh), two sprigs of parsley, and half a bay-leaf; simmer for fifteen minutes; strain through a scalded cloth; replace on the fire; add a piece of glaze as large as a hazel-nut, or a tablespoonful of strong meat-gravy, just enough to give it the shade of *palest* café au lait; thicken with two yolks of eggs, as for Allemande sauce. All articles served with this sauce are termed *à la Villeroi*. It differs.from d'Uxelles only in having no ham, nor acidity from the lemon; also, all flavor of onion is omitted.

III.

Suprème sauce gives its name to several dishes dear to epicures—suprême de volaille, suprême de Toulouse, etc. It is made with a pint of thick white sauce, a pint of very strong chicken broth, four stalks of parsley, and six white pepper-corns, boiled down to half a pint. Stir sauce and broth together until thoroughly blended, then boil rapidly down till thick again, taking great care it does not burn. Add one gill of double cream, and half a saltspoonful of salt (if the stock was already seasoned). Boil up till thick enough *to mask the back of a spoon*, strain, and the last thing add a small teaspoonful of lemon juice.

When the white sauce has to be made expressly for the suprême, it is easier to use

strong chicken broth in place of ordinary
white stock ; then it is not necessary to add
it after. The term "to mask the back of a
spoon " is a common one to indicate the proper thickness for sauces, but to the untrained
eye it may not be easy to decide just what
"masking" means. Most sauces should be
thin enough to run quite freely from the
spoon, yet not so thin as to leave the color
of the spoon visible through the coating of
sauce it will retain if it be dipped into it ;
there should be a thin *opaque* coating or
"mask" to the back of the spoon. Sauce of
this thickness is produced by using one ounce
(exact weight) of flour of fine quality to half
a pint of liquid. Meat, fish, or vegetables
over which sauce of this consistency has
been poured will be quite masked, but the
sauce will not be too thick to serve readily
with a spoon. This consistency is worth
some practice to attain, for it is the perfection of sauce-making.

White sauce, when intended for the foundation of others, it must be observed, is made twice as thick, to allow for the addition of cream, wine, or stock. The only advantage in a private family of making it thus thick is when, perhaps, two or three sauces are needed for a dinner; for example, a plain white sauce for a vegetable, caper, lobster, or cardinal for other purposes, and perhaps poulette, d'Uxelles, or other pale sauce for an entrée; but when one sauce only is required, it is best to make that one from the beginning; that is to say, make white sauce with the additions that form it into Allemande, suprême, or whatever you require.

Ste. Ménehould Sauce is in these days chiefly associated with "pigs' feet à la Ste. Ménehould," but is good for several purposes. It is simply half a pint of white sauce into which a dozen bruised mushrooms, a gill of the mushroom liquor, a large teaspoonful of finely chopped chives, with the sixth of a saltspoonful of pepper and one of salt are allowed to simmer until the sauce is the same thickness as before the addition of the mush-room liquor; that is to say, thick enough to mask the spoon. Strain, return to the sauce-pan, and add a teaspoonful of finely chopped sage leaves, if for pigs' feet, or parsley for other purposes; boil once, add half a teaspoon-ful of lemon juice, and the sauce is ready.

Béarnaise Sauce.—This is one of the most difficult sauces to make, on account of the danger of the eggs curdling; but by the following method the work is rendered more sure than by the usual plan. It has been said that the terrors of a cook are Béarnaise sauce and omelette soufflée, but neither is really difficult; great care only is necessary for success with each.

Chop four shallots fine, put them into a saucepan with half a gill of Tarragon vine-gar and half a gill of plain vinegar; boil till reduced to one tablespoonful; then add one gill of white sauce, mixing well. Stand the saucepan in another of boiling water; then add, one at a time, three yolks of eggs, beating each one well in before adding another, *and on no account let the sauce boil.* Remove the saucepan from the fire when the eggs are all in and show signs of thickening. Have ready three ounces of butter cut into small pieces; drop one in at a time, and with an egg-whisk beat the sauce till the butter is blended; then add another piece, and so on, till all the butter is used. If added too quickly the butter will oil, therefore great care must be taken to see one piece entirely blend before adding another. The butter will probably salt the sauce enough, but if not, add a very little salt. This sauce should have the appearance of a Welsh-rabbit when ready to spread; in other words, it should be very thick, smooth, and dark yellow.

Soubise. — This sauce, which transforms ordinary mutton-chops into "côtelettes à la Soubise," is very easily made. Boil half a dozen Bermuda onions (medium size) in milk till quite tender; press out all the milk; chop them as fine as possible; sprinkle a quarter of a saltspoonful of white pepper and one of salt over them; then stir them with a tablespoonful of butter into half a pint of white sauce. If the onions should thin the sauce too much (they are sometimes very watery), thicken with a yolk of egg, or blend a teaspoonful of flour with the butter before stirring it in. Boil the sauce three minutes. Needless to say, if the yolk of egg is added, it must be beaten in after the sauce is removed from the stove, and only allowed to thicken, not boil.

The sauces so far given are what French cooks call "grand sauces." They are the most important part of the dish with which they are served, and, as we have seen, give the name to it. There are numberless other sauces of which the white sauce is parent that are, however, not indispensable to the dish they are served with—by which I mean a boiled fish may be served with oyster sauce or Dutch sauce, the sauce being in this case simply the adjunct.

A dessertspoonful of capers put into half a pint of white sauce, with a teaspoonful of the vinegar, makes caper sauce.

Celery sauce is, again, white sauce with the pulp of boiled celery. Boil the white part of four heads of celery (sliced thin) in milk till it will mash; this will take an hour, perhaps more; then rub the pulp through a coarse sieve, and stir it into half a pint of white sauce made with half rich cream.

Oyster sauce is white sauce made by using the oyster liquor instead of stock. The oysters should be bearded, just allowed to plump in the liquor, which must then be strained for the sauce, using a gill of it with a gill of thick cream to make half a pint; for this quantity a dozen and a half of small oysters will be required.

Shrimp sauce, parsley sauce, lobster sauce, cucumber sauce, and all the family are white sauce with the addition of the ingredient naming it. Cucumber sauce, which is approved for fish, is made by grating a cucumber, and adding it, with the water from it, to some white sauce; boil till well flavored, and then strain. If too thin, boil till thick, stirring carefully.

For shrimp sauce canned shrimps serve very well indeed; they must be thrown for a minute into cold water, well stirred in it to remove superfluous salt, then drained, and dried on a cloth. Put a gill of shrimps to half a pint of béchamel made with fish stock, boil once, and stir in just enough essence of anchovy to make the sauce a pale shrimp pink.

Cardinal sauce is a handsome sauce for boiled fish. It is made by drying the coral from a lobster, then pounding it quite smooth, with one ounce of butter, until it is a perfectly smooth paste. Stir this into half a pint of béchamel. It should be a fine red when mixed; pass through a sieve, and add as much cayenne as will go on the end of the blade of a small penknife.

Hollandaise or Dutch sauce is best made in

the following way. There are other methods, but this one meets general approval, is
not difficult, and agrees with many who cannot possibly eat it when oil is used.

Make half a pint of drawn butter by melting one ounce of butter with one ounce of
flour over the fire; let them bubble together
(stirring the while) for one minute; then stir
in half a pint of boiling water and half a
teaspoonful of salt. So far, the making is
exactly the same as for white sauce, except
that water is used instead of cream and
stock. Boil once, then set the saucepan in
another of water, and break up an ounce of
butter into small pieces and add them; stir
briskly after each piece is added, and see it
blend before putting more. When all is in,
add the beaten yolks of five eggs, removing
the saucepan from the fire while doing it.
They must be very carefully and gradually
stirred in, and when well mixed returned to
the fire until they *begin* to thicken. The
eggs must be kept from curdling. Squeeze

in two teaspoonfuls of lemon juice, and add just a dust of cayenne. This should be a thick, yellow, custard-like sauce, and have a perceptible acidity without being sour.

IV.

BROWN SAUCES.

It has been already stated that the family of brown sauces, like the white, have one parent, *Espagnole*, or Spanish sauce, which is the foundation for Châteaubriand, Financière, Robert, Poivrade, Piquante, and other sauces. Ordinary brown sauce, like ordinary white, is often made without stock—simply an ounce of flour, one of butter, browned together, and half a pint of boiling water added, then boiled till thick and smooth. But it may be safely said that in high-class dark sauces water should play no part; its place must be taken by stock of good quality, which is often enriched by reducing or adding glaze.

The characteristics of finely made Spanish sauce are a clear beautiful brown, by no

3

means approaching black, absolute freedom from grease, and a fine high flavor, so well blended that no particular spice or herb can be detected. Spanish sauce is made as follows: Wash, peel, and cut small six mushrooms (or a dessertspoonful of mushroom powder), one small carrot, one small onion, and one shallot; dry them, and fry them a fine brown in a tablespoonful of butter, but do not let them burn; drain off the butter. Melt in a copper saucepan two ounces of butter and two ounces of flour, stir them together over the fire till of a pale bright brown, then add a pint of stock, the fried vegetables, and a gill of tomato sauce; let all gently simmer for half an hour with the cover off. Strain through a fine sieve. When Spanish sauce is to be served without any addition, and not as a foundation, a wineglass of sherry is used and the same quantity of stock omitted.

It becomes Châteaubriand by the addition of a wineglass of sherry reduced to half a

glass by boiling in a tiny saucepan, a dessertspoonful of fresh parsley very finely chopped,
and the juice of half a small lemon. These
must be added to *one third* the quantity of
Espagnole, or Spanish sauce, given in the
foregoing recipe. Then stir in gradually,
bit by bit, one ounce of butter, letting each
piece blend before adding more.

I have said here and elsewhere, " the juice
of half a small lemon.". Yet I would caution the reader to squeeze it in gradually,
because some lemons are intensely sour, and
a very few drops of juice from such go far-
ther than that of the whole half of an average lemon. Châteaubriand sauce is by no
means acid; there must be only a just perceptible dash of acidity, and only so much
lemon juice used as will give it zest. Piquante sauce is different; there should be
acidity enough to provoke appetite; yet
even this should be by no means sour.

To make *Piquante sauce*, chop a shallot
fine, put it, with a tablespoonful of vinegar,

into a very small saucepan; let them stew
together until the vinegar is *entirely absorbed*, but do not let it burn.   Then add to
it half a pint of Spanish sauce and a gill of
stock, with a bay-leaf and a sprig of thyme;
cook very gently ten minutes, remove the
thyme and bay-leaf, and add a dessertspoonful of chopped pickled cucumber, a teaspoonful of capers, and a dessertspoonful of *finely*
chopped parsley.   Simmer very slowly ten
minutes more; then add enough cayenne to
lay on the tip of a penknife blade.

Poivrade resembles piquante sauce very
closely, differing from it, however, by the
addition of wine and higher flavoring.   To
make it, fry an onion and a small carrot cut
fine, a tomato sliced, and an ounce of lean
ham in two ounces of butter; let them
brown slightly; then add to them half a
pint of claret, a bouquet of herbs, two cloves,
and six peppercorns; let them simmer till
the wine is reduced one half; then add half
a pint of good Spanish sauce, boil gently ten

minutes, strain, and serve very hot. A true French poivrade has a *soupçon* of garlic, obtained by rubbing a crust on a clove of it, and simmering it in the sauce before straining it; but although many would like the scarcely perceptible zest imparted by this cautious use of garlic, no one should try the experiment unless sure of her company.

A "bouquet of herbs" always means two sprigs of parsley, one of thyme, one of marjoram, and a bay-leaf, so rolled together (the bay-leaf in the middle) and tied that there is no difficulty in removing it from any dish which is not to be strained.

The well-known *Bordelaise sauce* is simply Spanish sauce with the addition of white wine and shallots. Scald a tablespoonful of chopped shallots; put them to half a pint of Chablis, Sauterne, or any similar white wine; let the wine reduce to one gill; then mix with it half a pint of Spanish sauce and the sixth part of a saltspoonful of pepper. Strain and serve.

Robert sauce, that excellent adjunct to beefsteak, varies again from Bordelaise, vinegar and mustard and fried onions taking the place of the wine and shallot. Chop three medium-sized onions quite fine; fry them in a tablespoonful of butter until they are a clear yellowish - brown, stirring them constantly as they fry; drain them, and put them to a half - pint of Spanish sauce, to which you add a wineglass of stock (to allow for boiling away); simmer gently twenty minutes; add a pinch of pepper; strain; then mix a teaspoonful of vinegar in a cup with a teaspoonful of mustard; stir this into the sauce.

Sauce à la Normande is one of the most delicious sauces for baked fish of any kind, although usually associated with sole. To half a pint of Spanish sauce add a dozen mushrooms sliced in half, a dozen small oysters with the beards removed, and a dozen crawfish, if they are to be had, or their place may be taken by a tablespoonful of shrimps picked (canned shrimps, washed and dried, answer very well), one tablespoonful of essence of anchovy, and just a dust of Cayenne pepper.

Light *Normande* is made by using béchamel instead of Spanish sauce, adding all the other materials; it is then a pale salmon-colored sauce, excellent for boiled fish.

A favorite English sauce for fish, which is also brown or pink, according to whether it is intended for baked or boiled fish, is the *Downton sauce.* To three quarters of a pint of béchamel add a dessertspoonful of anchovy essence and a small wineglass of sherry, mix well, and serve.

Orange sauce for game is made with half a pint of Spanish sauce boiled five minutes to make it rather thicker than usual, the juice of three sweet oranges, and the peel of one. This peel must be so thinly pared as to be transparent. Boil this peel half an hour in water, then shred it into fine even strips half an inch long, and not thicker than broom straw. Stew this shredded peel another half-hour in a gill of stock, with a

scant teaspoonful of sugar; then add it to
the sauce, with half a saltspoonful of salt,
and boil five minutes.

Matelote may come in with the brown
sauces, although it is not made with Spanish
sauce as a foundation, but only with strong
stock. It is used to simmer fish in when directed to be *à la matelote*, and if it were already thickened the whole would burn. It
is made as follows: Half a pint of Sauterne
or Chablis, half a pint of rich stock, two bay-
leaves, three leaves of tarragon, chervil, and
chive, a scant saltspoonful of salt, a quarter
one of pepper; simmer these until reduced
to one half-pint. A *touch* of garlic is indispensable to the true matelote, but when used
it must be done with the greatest caution; a
fork stuck into a clove of it, then stirred in
the sauce (the fork, when withdrawn, not the
garlic), or a crust rubbed once across a piece of
it, is the only way in which it should be used.

Like the white sauces, the family of brown
ones is very large, but I have given those

which require special directions. Others are simply Spanish sauce with the addition of the ingredient which gives its name to it, as brown oyster sauce is simply Spanish sauce with oysters, celery sauce, mushroom sauce, and so on. It should always be remembered that the consistency must be preserved; that is to say, except when special mention is made of the sauce being thinner, it should " mask the spoon," and if the addition made to it is of a kind to dilute it, as mushrooms and part of their liquor, it must be rapidly boiled down to the original thickness. In the same way, when ingredients have to be simmered in the sauce—and this is very often the case —then a wineglassful or half one of broth or stock should be allowed for the wasting.

In the next chapter we will make acquaintance with the miscellaneous sauces which are not built on the foundation of either white or brown sauce. These are chiefly cold sauces, although served with hot dishes at times, as Tartare, Remoulade, etc.

V.

COLD dishes, which are such a pleasing feature of foreign cookery, are much neglected with us, at least in private kitchens, or they are limited to two or three articles served in mayonnaise, or a galantine, yet the dishes which the French call *chaud-froids* are both delicious and ornamental, and it only requires a little taste, care, and *perfect sauce* to convert the ordinary cold chicken, .turkey, or game into an elaborate and choice dish.

Among cold sauces, of course mayonnaise, both green, red, and yellow, reigns supreme; indeed, of late years it has become almost hackneyed. Yet no work on choice eating would be complete without the different forms of mayonnaise.

Mayonnaise is one of those sauces in which everything depends on care, and very little on skill, and yet some women have quite a reputation for making it among their friends who often declare how unsuccessful their own efforts have been, and that to succeed is a gift. It is not as a novelty, therefore, that the manner of making it is given here, but that those who believe they have not the "magic fingers" may take courage and try again.

First of all let me explain what seems to puzzle many. I have been frequently asked, " How much oil can I use to two eggs?" the answer is, "As much as you choose;" or, again, " How many eggs ought I to take to a quart of oil?" again the answer is, " One, two, three, or four." The egg is only a foundation, and mayonnaise will " come " no better with two yolks than one, although some *chefs* consider it keeps better when two eggs are used to a pint of oil.

A cool room is always insisted on for making the sauce, but to the amateur I say, oil, eggs, and bowl also, should be put in the ice-box until well chilled, and even then mishaps may come from using a warm spoon from a hot kitchen drawer or closet.; that, therefore, must be cool also. Of course it is often suc-cessfully made with only the usual precau-tion of a cool room, but with everything well chilled it is hard to fail.

If very little of the sauce is wanted, one yolk of egg will be better than two. Sepa-rate the yolks very carefully, allowing not a speck of white to remain; remove also the germ which is attached to the yolk. *Stir the yolk at least a minute before* beginning to add oil; then arrange your bottle or a sharp-spouted pitcher in your left hand so that it rests on the edge of the bowl, and you can keep up a pretty steady drop, drop, into the egg, while you stir with your right steadily. The oil must be added drop by drop, but this does not mean a drop every two or three minutes; you may add a drop to every one or two circuits of the spoon. The reason for adding it slowly is that each drop may form an emulsion with the egg before more goes in. After two or three minutes look carefully at the mixture; if it has not begun to look pale and opaque, but retains a dark, oily appearance, stir it steadily for two minutes, and then add oil slowly, drop by drop, stirring all the time. If it has not now begun to thicken, it probably will not; but the materials are not lost. Put the yolk of another egg into a cool bowl, and begin again using the egg and oil you have already mixed, in place of fresh oil. When this is all used, proceed with the oil (it is hoped, however, that the work will have proceeded without the necessity for beginning afresh). When the mayonnaise becomes quite thick, use a few drops of vinegar to thin it; then more oil, until sufficient sauce is made. Then white pepper and salt should be added for seasoning. The vinegar used should be very strong, so that very little of it will be sufficient to give the necessary acidity, without making it too thin. This is especially the case when the sauce is required to mask salad. It should for this purpose be set on ice until firm, but in all·cases be kept cold. The best mayonnaise, left in a warm kitchen, would separate and become oily. The stirring must be steady and constant, and the task must not be left until completed.

Mayonnaise is the basis of several other sauces, so that in accomplishing it a great deal is done.

Green mayonnaise is made by dropping a bunch of parsley into boiling water, and in a minute or two, when it becomes intensely green, take it up, pound it in a mortar, and then through a sieve. Use as much pulp as will color the sauce a delicate green.

Red mayonnaise, used for cardinal salad and other purposes, is made by pounding lobster coral very fine and stirring it in. It must not be forgotten that anything added to mayonnaise must be ice-cold.

Aspic mayonnaise is another form of the sauce, used in dressing cold dishes, and while more delicious than the usual sauce, will keep its form for hours after the dish is dressed. It is absolutely necessary to prepare it on ice. Put half a pint of stiff aspic jelly into a bowl set in cracked ice, whisk it with an egg-beater until it is a white froth (usually the motion will melt it, but to save labor it may be set in lukewarm water to soften, then beaten, but no oil must be added until it is again ice-cold froth); then beat in very gradually a quarter of a pint of olive oil and a tablespoonful of tarragon vinegar, proceeding with the same care as for the usual mayonnaise; add a saltspoonful of salt, a pinch of pepper, and the same of powdered sugar.

Norwegian sauce is preferred by many to Tartare for some purposes, and is made by adding *freshly* grated horseradish to mayonnaise in the proportion of two tablespoonfuls to half a pint.

Tartare sauce is mayonnaise with the addition of mustard, chives, pickles, and tarragon, chopped. As usually served, it has only mustard and capers or chopped cucumber, but for those to whom a slight flavor of onion is not disagreeable, chives should be added. To half a pint of mayonnaise use a teaspoonful of dry mustard mixed with two of tarragon vinegar, then stir into the sauce. To this add a tablespoonful either of capers or chopped pickled cucumber; this is the usual Tartare sauce; but the French recipe is a tablespoonful of very finely chopped chives, a teaspoonful each of fresh tarragon and chervil in place of the pickles.

Cold cucumber sauce is mayonnaise with an equal quantity of grated cucumber, drained, pressed, and stirred into it, with a saltspoonful of salt and a few drops of very strong vinegar.

Horseradish sauce is a very good sauce for hot or cold beef, roast or boiled. Grate three tablespoonfuls of horseradish fine, put to it a teaspoonful of sugar, one of salt, and one of vinegar, or a tablespoonful of Chablis wine; let them soak an hour or two, and the last thing before serving stir in four table-spoonfuls of cream that is whipped very solid. A half-teaspoonful of dry mustard is sometimes mixed with the horseradish, but that is a matter of taste. When the sauce is to be served hot, two yolks of egg and two tablespoonfuls of water must be substituted for cream, which would curdle. The water, horseradish, etc., must first come to the boiling-point, then the eggs added gradually, and just allowed to thicken, not to boil.

Mint Sauce.—Take only the young, tender leaves, not a bit of stem, and chop very fine indeed. To two tablespoonfuls add a table-spoonful and a half of brown sugar and three of vinegar. It should be quite thick, not as we so often see it—vinegar with a few bits of mint floating around.

Mint Jelly for masking cold lamb or cut-

4

lets.—Take two tablespoonfuls of Spanish
sauce, and dissolve in it a good teaspoonful
of gelatine softened in cold stock, a tablespoonful of aspic, and one of thick mint
sauce. If no aspic is ready, it is not worth
while to make for the small quantity needed ;
a teaspoonful of glaze, two of gelatine, and
half a wineglass of Sauterne may be dissolved together to take its place. No gelatine will be needed with the Spanish sauce
in this case.

Sweet sauces will be left until the desserts
are treated of.

VI.

SOUPS.

It is not proposed to give the soups to be found readily in most cooking-books in these pages, but only those less known or of peculiar excellence.

It is supposed that the reader understands the making of good beef or veal stock, and perhaps the usual way of clearing it. But since cooking has been studied scientifically, improvements on methods have been introduced; one of these is the clearing of soup with albumen of *meat* instead of egg. The advantages of this method are that the soup is strengthened and the flavor improved, while clearing with whites of eggs in the usual way, though greatly improving the appearance, tends to lessen the flavor of soup.

To clear Consommé with Beef. — Consommé is reduced stock, or stock made of extra strength. Carefully remove all fat from three pints of it when cold. It will, of course, be a stiff jelly. Chop fine an onion, a carrot, and a turnip. Chop half a pound of lean beef from which all fat is removed; this is best put through a chopping-machine, as it must be very fine. Put the consommé, meat, and vegetables into a saucepan. Stir them briskly till just on the boiling-point. Remove the spoon, let the soup boil up well one minute. It should now be clear. Take a clean cloth, fix it on a soup stand or in a colander, pour boiling water through it, to warm it thoroughly; throw the water away, and pour the soup gently through the cloth twice; do not press or stir it. It will be beautifully clear and of excellent color. It is now ready to serve for a variety of soups, named according to what is served in them.

Consommé à la Rachel.—This is consommé to which is added tiny quenelles made in egg-spoons, and colored red, green, and black.

Quenelle meat is made from the uncooked breast of chicken or game, the backs of hares or rabbits (or it may be made for certain purposes of fish or very white veal), first chopped, and then pounded in a mortar until it is a perfectly smooth paste. Mere chopped meat is not what is required; it must be fine enough to go through a sieve. For Consommé à la Rachel, however, the breast of chicken is necessary. Take four ounces of chicken, free from skin and sinew; pound it until quite smooth; the more it is pounded the better it is. Mix with it thick cream, a scant saltspoonful of salt, very little pepper, and half a beaten egg, until it is a softish paste, yet firm enough to mould; mix thoroughly. Now try a little by poaching in a teaspoon; that is, fill a teaspoon with the mixture, pressing it in form, then drop it into boiling water for three minutes. Open the quenelle and taste it; if it is creamy, light, and well flavored, it is right, but if there is the least toughness, add a little more cream to the mixture. Notice also the seasoning; if more salt is needed, add it carefully, and try again, till you have the quenelle mixture just right, that is to say, creamy, light, very tender, yet keeping its form. At present quenelles as entrées or for soups form such an important part of fine cooking that it is worth while to get the mixture perfect for other purposes than the present.

Having your quenelle meat ready, proceed to vary it as follows, allowing one quenelle of each color to each guest: For the green quenelles use sufficient pounded tarragon to color one third the meat delicately. For the second use sufficient lobster coral pounded to redden it. The third must be made dark with pounded truffles. Great care must be taken to keep the three portions separate, so that one color may not injure the other. To form them use two very small coffeespoons or eggspoons, as the quenelles should not be larger than *small* olives; butter the spoons slightly, and when formed drop each for one or two minutes into boiling pale-colored stock. Drop them, as they are done, into cold water, in which they must be kept until you are ready to use them. When the soup is to be served, drain them, lay the number required in the tureen, and pour the boiling consommé on them. They will not require heating in the soup. It may be observed that raw spinach pounded and rubbed through a sieve, and boiled red beet, may be used to color the meat green and red, and the rest left white. The consommé is then called Consommé d'Orleans.

Consommé aux Œufs filés.—Put one quart of cleared consommé to boil. Mix one egg, one dessertspoonful of flour, one tablespoonful of milk, a pinch between forefinger and thumb of salt, and a dust of pepper, into a batter, rub a nutmeg once back and forth over the grater, and stir. When the soup boils, pass this batter through a fine strainer into it. It should look like threads.

Consommé à la Sévigné. — Pound two

ounces of breast of cooked chicken until it will pass through a wide sieve. Mix with it two eggs, three tablespoonfuls of milk, twelve drops of almond essence, a scant saltspoonful of salt, as much nutmeg as will go on the end of a penknife blade, and a dust of cayenne. When well blended, fill three or four small round muffin pans, well greased, and steam slowly twenty minutes, or until set. Turn out very carefully; let them cool; then cut them into fancy shapes, and serve in one quart of boiling consommé. A few asparagus points boiled until just tender, but not mushy, are to be dropped in the last thing.

Potage à la Hollandaise.—For this will be required one quart of veal or chicken stock, two ounces of butter, one ounce of flour, four yolks of eggs, half a pint of cream, one gill of green peas, one gill of boiled carrots, one gill of boiled cucumber, one teaspoonful of fresh tarragon chopped fine, one teaspoonful of sugar, and one teaspoonful of salt. Trim the carrots and cucumber with a very small scoop or cutter the size and shape of peas; cook them just tender, and no more, in boiling water. Put the stock on to boil; skim if necessary; add the salt and sugar. Break the eggs into a bowl, add the cream to them, and beat them till well mixed. This forms a "liaison." Make the butter and flour into a paste in a bowl, pour half a gill of cold stock to it, then enough hot stock to dissolve it; when mixed smooth, stir it into the boiling stock, let it boil, then remove from the fire, and stir in very carefully, to prevent curdling, the liaison of eggs and cream; let it come to the boiling-point, but not boil, or it will curdle. Strain it into a clean stew-pan, and add the vegetables; let all get hot together; then strew in the tarragon.

Chestnut Soup (*purée de marrons*).—Slit twenty-five large chestnuts at each end, put them in boiling water, and boil ten minutes. Drop them into cold water, and remove both the outer and inner skin. Melt three ounces of butter in a saucepan, put in the chestnuts, and sauté (toss them about) for a few minutes, but do not brown them; then add a pint and a half of rich white stock, and let the nuts boil in it until very tender, when they must be rubbed through a fine sieve. Boil up again, add half a pint of cream, a teaspoonful of powdered sugar, a teaspoonful of salt (less if the stock be salted), and a pinch of pepper.

Princess Soup.—Cut a chicken in pieces; wash it; butter a stewpan, put in the chicken with a blade of mace, an onion, a bay-leaf, and twelve white peppercorns. Let this simmer, *closely covered*, ten minutes, shaking it often to prevent its browning; then put to it two quarts of hot veal stock, and simmer one hour. Put into another stewpan two ounces of flour and two ounces of butter; stir them together, and let them bubble once, then strain the liquor from the chicken to it; stir well, and cook a few minutes. Take the white meat from the bones of the chicken, pound it in a mortar very fine, stir it to the stock, then rub through a soup strainer; add just before serving half a pint of fresh cream and the juice of half a lemon. This soup must be made hot, but not boil, after the chicken pulp and cream are added.

Potage à la Royale.—Boil two ounces of macaroni till tender, but not broken; throw it into cold water. Put three pints of white stock to boil; cut the macaroni into lengths half an inch long; beat three yolks of eggs in a bowl with a gill of cream; throw the macaroni into the soup; when it boils, remove from the fire, add the cream and eggs and an ounce of grated Parmesan cheese; stir till the soup reaches the boiling-point, but by no means let it boil, after the cream and eggs are added, or it will be spoiled. Salt soup always in the proportion of a moderate teaspoonful of salt to the quart; if the stock is seasoned, only add salt for the cream, eggs, etc. Use just a suspicion of cayenne. In making soup to which eggs are added, the utmost care is required, yet not any more than in making custard. The main point is to let the eggs come near enough to the boiling-point to thicken, yet far enough from it not to curdle. This a little patience will accomplish by watching and removing the saucepan for a few seconds as the boiling-point approaches, then returning it; do this once or twice, till the opaque, creamy appearance shows the eggs are done.

VII.

INSTEAD of giving recipes for cooking fish whole, for which excellent directions are to be found in several modern cookery books, recipes for fish entrées will be substituted. They are now frequently served at the fish course, and by their convenience and economy, as well as the variety they afford, are likely to grow in favor. Another point for them is that they can often be made hours before, and simply heated when needed, thus relieving the cook of the most critical part of her work at the time when she needs her attention free.

Some of these entrées will be more suited for breakfast, luncheon, or supper dishes than to precede a heavy dinner, such, for instance, as the preparations of oysters when they have been also served before soup; but the recipes are included here for their intrinsic worth.

Fillets of Cod à la Normande.—Butter a tin dish, lay on it three slices of cod moderately thick (an inch to an inch and a half), pour over them one wineglass of white wine, place a buttered paper over them, and bake in a moderate oven fifteen minutes. Reduce another glass of wine in a stewpan by simmering, add to it half a pint of white sauce, twelve small oysters, bearded and blanched, twelve small quenelles,* and twelve button mushrooms. Season with pepper and salt. Simmer one minute only, or the oysters will harden. Place the slices of fish on a hot dish, pour the sauce over them, place the oysters, mushrooms, and quenelles in groups in the corners of the dish.

Lobster Soufflées.—Cut up the meat of a boiled hen lobster into neat dice, showing as

---

* See Quenelles in No. VI.

much of the red as possible. Prepare as many small ramekin or soufflée cases as may be required by pinning bands of writing-paper round them two to three inches higher than the case. Take three tablespoonfuls of mayonnaise, half a pint of stiff aspic jelly, and a gill of tomato sauce in which a teaspoonful of gelatine has been dissolved. Every utensil used must be ice-cold, the jelly must be quite cold, but not set. Put the tomato sauce, the jelly, and the mayonnaise (which should be left on the ice till the last thing) into a bowl set in another bowl of pounded ice; whisk them together until they begin to look white; then stir the lobster in it, with a teaspoonful of very finely chopped chervil and tarragon; fill the soufflée cases, piling the dressing high; put them on a dish on ice. When they are "set," carefully remove the paper bands, sprinkle a little dried and sifted lobster coral over the tops, and serve.

Coquilles of Prawns.—Pick the shells

from four dozen prawns; mix with one third the quantity of mushrooms slightly stewed in a tablespoonful of butter and a saltspoonful of salt (the mushrooms must not be brown); add. four tablespoonfuls of Allemande sauce ;* fill the shells, which must be well buttered, dress each over with fine bread crumbs which have been carefully fried a golden brown; put them in a cool oven twenty minutes, only get thoroughly hot, but not to cook.

Coquilles of Salmon or Halibut. — Take one pound of cold halibut or salmon; break it into small pieces; put it in a stewpan with half a saltspoonful of salt and a tiny pinch of pepper, and half a pint of white sauce, a tablespoonful of very thick cream, and a teaspoonful of anchovy sauce; stir well, and let all get hot. Butter some shells, sprinkle over with a few fried crumbs, fill with the mixture, cover with the fried

---

* See directions in No. II.

crumbs, and put them in the oven to get thoroughly hot. Serve on a napkin.

Salmon en Papillotes.—Cut some slices of salmon into cutlets the right size for serving, make paper cases to fit them, then cover each slice with the following mixture: two tablespoonfuls of salad oil beaten with the yolk of an egg, one teaspoonful of parsley chopped, one shallot chopped, and one anchovy (all these must be chopped as finely as possible), a half-saltspoonful of salt, and a grain of cayenne; mix, spread on the fish, envelop each piece in a well-buttered case, fasten up (by pinching the paper well), and bake half an hour. Serve in the papers.

Fillet of Sole à la Normande.—In speaking of sole, one of course means the flounder, which is coming to be called the American sole, and when filleted does make a fair substitute for the real thing, and it is suitable for cooking in every way that the English sole can be used, except whole. A boiled flounder without filleting, or a flounder fried

5

whole, as is so often done with sole, would
be very coarse. Fillet two flounders (in
cities this will be done by the fishmonger,
but in the country it may have to be done
in the kitchen, therefore directions for doing
it will be appended), lay the fillets, neatly
trimmed and shaped, into a thickly buttered
pan or dish—either fire-proof porcelain or
any other that can go to table—pour over
them a glass of sherry and four tablespoonfuls of consommé; cover with oiled paper,
and bake ten minutes in a moderate oven;
take out the pan, pour over the fillets half a
pint of *sauce Normande;* return to the oven
for five minutes, and serve in the pan.

Sole à l'Horly.—Make a frying batter
thus: mix one tablespoonful of milk with
two ounces of flour and a tablespoonful of
salad oil to a smooth paste; then add two
yolks of eggs, and the whites whipped firm,
with a quarter of a saltspoonful of salt; mix
with an upward movement of the spoon, so
as not to deaden the whites of eggs. Set it

aside while you prepare the sole. Mix a tablespoonful of salad oil, a teaspoonful of Chili vinegar, a teaspoonful of tarragon vinegar, a teaspoonful of parsley and one of onion chopped exceedingly fine, a scant saltspoonful of salt, and a quarter one of pepper. Mix all together, then cut the fillets in half, trimming away all ragged appearance, and lay them for fifteen minutes in the mixture (called a marinade); take them out, drain them on a sieve, and then dip each fillet in the batter. This batter should be just thick enough to coat the fish and run slowly off, not cling in a thick paste round it. A French rule for testing the thickness of frying batter is to dip a spoon in it and then let a drop run off the end on a plate; if it drops freely, yet keeps a beadlike form, it is right. Fry each fillet in a wire basket three minutes in very hot deep fat. Serve with fried parsley.

Turbans of Sole à la Rouennaise. — As these require a little of the same mixture as would be used for lobster cutlets or croquettes, it is good management to have them when lobster is required for something else. The mixture for the cutlets is made as follows (less than a fourth of it would be required for the turbans): remove all the flesh from a boiled hen lobster; chop it small; wash, dry, and pound the coral, with an ounce of butter; take one gill of white sauce, mix the lobster coral and a tablespoonful of cream with it, and boil five minutes; mix in the lobster with a little salt (unless the lobster is salt enough) and a grain of cayenne. This made into cutlets, egged, crumbed, and fried, is excellent, but our purpose now is to use it for stuffing. Take as many fillets of sole as required, spread the lobster mixture on each, roll them up, run a toothpick through them to keep them in shape; trim till each will stand; put them on a buttered baking-sheet, cover with buttered paper, and bake ten minutes. Chop up two truffles, two hard-boiled yolks of eggs, and a tablespoonful of parsley, each chopped separately. Take

up the turbans, pour over them half a pint of
cardinal sauce, and ornament the turbans,
one with the truffles, one with the yolk of
egg, and one with parsley; so on alternately.

Directions for Filleting Flounders.—Take
a sharp knife, cut away the fins all round the
fish, and split the flounder right down the
middle of the back, then run the knife carefully between the flesh and bones, going towards the edge. You have now detached
one quarter of the flesh from the bone; do
the other half in the same way, and when
the back is thus entirely loose from the bone,
turn the fish over and do the same with the
other side. You will now find you can remove the bone whole from the fish, detach-
ing, as you do so, any flesh still retaining the
bone. Then you have two halves of the fish,
and you have four quarters of solid fish. To
remove the skin, take the tail end firmly between the thumb and forefinger of the left
hand, hold the skin side downward on the
board, and with your knife make an incision

across the flesh, then, keeping the skin firmly between your thumb and finger, *push* the knife between it and the flesh, slightly humoring it to prevent tearing the flesh. The skin parts quite easily, but no attempt must be made to *cut* the fish from it.

VIII.

Oysters à la · Villeroi.—Scald (or blanch) some large oysters, dry them, then drop them into some *very thick* Villeroi sauce,* let them get hot in it, but not boil. Take them out one by one; be sure they are thickly coated with the sauce; have a large dish heaped with sifted crumbs or cracker meal; as you lift each oyster from the sauce lay it on the meal, turn it gently over in the meal, so that a light coat adheres, and the sauce is by no means rubbed off. Place them on an oiled plate where they will get quite cold, so that the sauce may chill and form a whitish glaze under the crumbs. Beat two eggs with two tablespoonfuls of water, and when free from

---

* See No. II.

strings dip each oyster in the egg, using a small fork; let superfluous egg drip off for a moment, then lay the oyster again on a deep bed of cracker crumbs, cover well, pat very gently, and lay each as you do it on a dish sprinkled with them. Fry two minutes in very hot deep fat, being careful the oysters do not touch each other.

If I have made these directions as clear as I hope, it will be understood that each oyster has a rich creamy coating under the crumbs, and every effort must be made to avoid breaking the outer shell of egg and crumb. For this reason the fat should be heated to 400°. But although great care in handling is necessary, they are not difficult to succeed with when that care is given.

Oyster Kabobs.—There are two ways of preparing these dainties, and I give both. For those who cannot eat bacon the first will probably be acceptable. For kabobs of any kind, silver or plated skewers are proper, although very slender wooden ones may be used. Put in a stewpan a small onion chopped *very fine*, a dessertspoonful of parsley, and a dozen mushrooms, also chopped; let these fry one minute in a large tablespoonful of butter, add a dessertspoonful (scant) of flour, stir all together, then drop in as many fat oysters as are required; they must have been blanched in their own liquor and the beards removed; stir all round, and add three beaten yolks of eggs, one at a time, taking care they do not curdle, but get just thick enough to cling round the oyster. String six oysters on each little skewer, basting with the sauce wherever it does not adhere; let each skewer cool, then roll the whole in beaten eggs and abundant cracker meal, so that the skewer will seem to be run through a sausage lengthwise. Fry two minutes in very hot deep fat, serve on a napkin; allow one skewer to each person. Two minutes, if the fat be sufficiently hot, will fry oysters a pale yellow-brown. They should never take longer than this, for oysters harden and shrink if overdone in the least. For this reason the use of a pyrometer, when possible, saves mistakes and trouble. Such articles as oysters, smelts, or any small things, should be fried at a temperature of 380° to 400°. It must be remembered that all fried articles darken after they leave the frying-kettle, and therefore a very pale yellow becomes a golden color on the dish.

Kabobs No. 2.—This is the recipe given by the author of the well-known Pytchley Books, and is admirable. Take the beards from as many fat, fair-sized oysters as required. You require bacon of which the fat is thick enough through to allow of circles being cut from the slices as large as the oysters. Cut the bacon very thin, get a cutter the size of the oysters, trim them with it, then cut eight circles of bacon for six oysters. Put first a piece of bacon, then an oyster, then more bacon, on each little skewer, till there are six oysters with a piece of bacon between each through the centre and one at each end ; string them very evenly. Take a very little cayenne on the tip of a knife and a saltspoonful of salt; mix this with two beaten eggs to which two tablespoonfuls of water have been added. Dip each skewer of kabobs in this; let them drip an instant, then lay them on a deep bed of crumbs or cracker meal. Cover them thoroughly, shake them, then dip again into the egg (if this has become full of crumbs strain it), and again lay them in the meal. Shake lightly again, and arrange each skewer of kabobs in a frying-basket, and fry two minutes.

I have spoken in the foregoing directions for "crumbing" of using *plenty* of meal, and experience tells me that the rule with those unfamiliar with proper methods is to use so little that a plateful would be considered *plenty*. With this quantity no good work can be done. You need to turn on to a board or dish at least a quart of crumbs, or a whole box of cracker meal. This will enable you to smother the article until every part is covered, instead of sprinkling a little

over and under (which generally falls off as
fast as put on, and leaves a surface yellow
with egg in parts), as you must do if a small
quantity only is used. All the meal that is
left must be carefully sifted and put away.
If the small masses of egg and crumb which
will be mixed with it are not sifted out the
cracker-meal cannot be used again. There
must also be plenty of egg used for dipping.

Oysters in Aspic.—For these dariole moulds
are needed, or the small fire-proof china soufflée cases which imitate paper may be used.
A dariole is a small straight-sided tin mould,
holding rather less than a gill. They will
be found at large house-furnishing stores, or
a tinman could easily make them, they being, in fact, like deep corn-muffin pans. If
they are made to order, avoid getting them
too large—three inches deep by two across
will be large enough. Fill these moulds with
aspic jelly nearly cold, set them on ice while
you prepare the oysters, which must be bearded and cooked till plump in butter, but not

allowed to color. When cool, cut them in half, throw them into some stiff béchamel,* which must be warmed till like thick cream, sprinkle with a dust of cayenne; lay the oysters to get cold, that the béchamel may harden on them. Scoop the centre very carefully out of the moulds of aspic, leaving a half-inch thickness all round, fill the centres with the oysters, pour in more aspic, cold, but not set, and put on ice for a few hours, or till ready to serve. The aspic from the centres should have been preserved and used to chop with more to garnish the dish. Turn the moulds out very carefully, and garnish with chopped aspic and watercress or parsley.

It is, of course, understood that béchamel sauce, cold, is like blanc-mange, and that anything coated with it will be enveloped in white jelly, not in a sticky white sauce. If béchamel does not become white jelly when cold the stock of which it is made is not stiff enough.

Lobster in Aspic is prepared as for salad,

* See No. II.

the solid meat cut in dice and rolled in mayonnaise, then in chopped chervil or parsley. Then proceed exactly as for the oysters.

Oysters à la Tartare.—The oyster-shells for serving oysters à la Tartare must be of good shape and exquisitely clean; therefore, when using oysters on the half-shell, always pick out any that may be deep yet stand well, and have a good shape; scald and scrub them, and keep for use. Scald as many fat oysters as required in their own liquor till firm—three minutes at boiling-point will usually do this; the oysters must be just plump, yet if underdone they will be flabby. Put them on ice, choose as many tiny leaves as you have oysters from the heart of a lettuce; they must all be of a size, or trimmed so, and the size only just large enough to line the shells without coming over them. Lay a leaf on each shell, cut each oyster in half, lay four halves in pyramid fashion on the lettuce leaf, and mask the top of each, just before serving, with Tartare sauce. Allow two to each person.

IX.

This little book does not pretend to go into what may be called the principles of cooking, except in so far as they are involved in the production of all choice cookery ; and where it is considered that a principle is little known or too little attended to, the effort will be made to give it emphasis by reiteration here.

By principles of cooking I mean the simple rules by which roasting, boiling, stewing, etc., are successfully accomplished. Any book or series of articles written a dozen years ago would have been of no real use without these rudiments, but within that period there have been cooking-schools started and cookery books written so exceedingly exact in directions that it will be unnecessary to repeat them in " Choice Cookery," which does not pretend to include family cooking.

For this reason the cooking of joints of meat will not be entered into. Nevertheless there are certain rudiments of cooking which are not dwelt on usually in books. They are taught in the cooking-schools, and those of my readers who have had the advantage of attending them will not need the instruction here given. But I meet with many women who devote much time to the art of cooking, and who have taught themselves by book and experiment all they know, who yet, when told to chop a small quantity of herbs very fine, will struggle and chop almost leaf by leaf in their faithful endeavor to carry out the direction. Others, less faithful, finding their method chops some parts fine and leaves some leaves almost whole, let it go at that, with the reflection that "that *must* do, as it would take all day" to get them all one degree of fineness. So, although it may seem almost too trivial a point to need mention, we will go into the matter of herb-chopping, lemon-grating, etc., that the simple operations may be performed easily and in a very short time.

To Chop Herbs.—Use the leaves only, never the stems; let them be fresh and crisp, or, if wilted, leave them in water for a time. Gather the leaves firmly between the thumb and three fingers of the left hand; shave them through with a sharp knife as you push them forward under it. (The process resembles chaff-cutting by hand machine.) Turn them round; gather them up again, and cut across them in the same way; then finish by chopping quickly, holding the point of the knife with the left hand and bringing it down on the little heap of herbs with the right, always gathering them together as fast as the chopping scatters them. Five minutes will chop a tablespoonful of mint or parsley almost to pulp. A sharp steel knife and a small board must be used, not the chopping-bowl.

6

French books often direct so much *fine herbs* to be used; English books mean the same thing when they call for "sweet herbs," and a mixture of one part marjoram, two parts thyme, and three parts parsley is meant by both.

The grating of a lemon is a most simple operation, and it may seem that every one must know how to do it; but this is far from being the case. As many dishes of curdled custards and sauces are caused by this fact, the right way in this case is very important. The object of using grated rind of lemon is to obtain the fragrance and flavor, which differ very greatly from any extracts, however good. Now the whole of the oil which contains this fragrance is at the surface—is, in fact, the yellow portion of the rind; therefore this, and only this, must be removed with the grater. The white part underneath is bitter, and will cause milk or cream to curdle, but it contains no particle of lemon flavor. Yet when lemon flavor is called for the lemon is often grated right down to the pulp in parts, while the yellow rind is left on in patches.

A lemon should be grated evenly, beginning at the end and working round it, using as small a surface of the grater as possible, to prevent waste. The habit of turning the lemon as you grate comes as easily as to turn an apple under the knife when peeling. Generally twice across the grater and back between each turn will remove all the essential oil, but, while guarding against grating too deeply, care must be taken to remove the whole of the yellow surface. A well-grated lemon should be exactly of the same shape as before, have no deep scores into the pith, and have an oily-looking surface.

Perhaps before proceeding to the preparation of the combination dishes known as made dishes or entrées, a few words may be useful to those readers whose ambition to accomplish results may cause them to defeat their own ends. To such I would say, go slowly; never attempt the more difficult thing until the simpler one is beyond chance of failure. Thus in following the instructions in this book the wiser women will have accomplished, perhaps, each week one or two things they may have selected, and it must not be forgotten the plan of the work is that one recipe shall serve as a key to many others.

A great many will very likely have delayed trying to make the sauces until the dish for which they will be required is given. This is a mistake, because it is less annoying to fail with a sauce with no dish depending on it, than, say, when you have decided to have sole *à la Villeroi*, the soles being ready, and fail with the sauce.

I hope that no failure will come to any one trying the recipes here given, but in some cases, especially in sauces thickened with eggs, a second's diverted attention may cause failure without fault of the cook. Therefore it is best to make single experiments when there is no danger of being disturbed, and when there is nothing else to be attended to. The successful result need never be lost, for in the case of sauces they can be reheated the next day in a bain-marie, or pan of hot water; the same with the soups, and, indeed, most other things, except soufflées and omelets.

But, above all things, never try a recipe for the first time the day you wish it to appear perfect on your table; try it long before, and if you fail, make the same thing over again, reading the directions very carefully; some trifling caution or precaution may have escaped you. No one ever learns to draw so simple a thing as a circle who is discouraged at the first bad curve, and leaves it for easier lines. Keep on at the thing you select to do until you succeed, always choosing *and perfecting* the easiest thing in each class first.

X

ENTRÉES.

Fillet of Beef. — This favorite dish with French and Americans may be roasted whole, or cut so as to serve individually. To roast it whole, it must be trimmed perfectly round, and either larded or not as taste may dictate. A fillet weighing four pounds should be roasted three quarters of an hour in a sharp oven. It may then be served *à la Châteaubriand* by pouring over it half a pint of the sauce of that name, with horseradish sauce, or brown mushroom sauce (brown sauce with mushrooms added).

To serve individually, fillets are prepared in the following way: Cut a fillet into eight slices three quarters of an inch thick; trim the slices into perfect circles, all exactly the same size; flatten them; put them in a hot pan, and sauté for seven or eight minutes in two ounces of butter; dress them round a dish, and pour over them the sauce from which the dish will take its name.

Filets de Bœuf à la Béarnaise.—Serve with half a pint of Béarnaise sauce.

Filets de Bœuf aux Champignons.—Dress as before; leave in the centre of the dish room for a mound of stewed mushrooms; pour over the fillets half a pint of rich brown sauce. Serve these dishes as soon as cooked: the meat is spoiled by waiting.

I have received several letters from readers living where lobster is only to be had in cans, asking if there is no substitute for the coral in making cardinal sauce. Canned lobster frequently contains a great deal of coral, which is as good for coloring and flavoring as the fresh. This can only be known, however, before opening, when the cans are of glass. The pulp of red beet-root passed through a sieve and added to white sauce or mayonnaise gives a beautiful red tint; but the flavor, while excellent for a salad or as vegetable sauce, would be unsuitable for serving with fish.

Grenadines of Beef with Mushrooms and Poivrade Sauce.—Take as many slices of fillet of beef, cut three quarters of an inch thick, as you require. Trim them to a pear shape, three and a half inches long and three wide at the broadest part. Lard these with bacon, and put them into a sauté pan with a gill of brown sauce and a glass of sherry (half the sauce if there are very few grenadines); let them cook gently for fifteen minutes. Dissolve a piece of glaze the size of a walnut by putting it in a cup which is set in boiling water; when dissolved, take up the grenadines, dish them in a circle, and glaze them (a brush is properly used for this purpose, but the glaze can be spread with a knife dipped in hot water). Fill the centre of the circle with a pyramid of small mushrooms mixed with a gill and a half of poivrade sauce.*

---

* See No. IV.

Fillets of Beef à la Grande-Bretagne.—Cut two pounds of fillet into neat slices an inch thick; slit them (with a small French boning-knife or small penknife) in such a way that you form a pocket in each the mouth or opening of which is smaller than the pocket itself. This can be done by laying the fillet flat on a board, laying your hand on the top of it, making a slit two inches wide, then with the point of the knife enlarging the slit inside, but not the entrance to it. The opening should extend half-way through; into this put a force-meat made of horserad-ish sauce* and macaroni boiled and cut fine. The force-meat must be used sparingly, so as not to increase materially the thickness of the fillet; fasten the opening of each with a wooden toothpick. Sauté these fillets for fifteen minutes; glaze them as directed in last recipe; arrange them in a circle, with a pyramid of tiny potato balls in the centre. Pour rich brown sauce round.

* See No. V.

Mutton Cutlets à la d' Uxelles.—Cut some cutlets from the neck of mutton, leaving two bones to each, trim very carefully, remove the upper part of one bone, split the cutlets without separating them at the bone, spread some thick d'Uxelles sauce* inside, fold the cutlets together, run a toothpick through them, and broil for four minutes on each side over a hot fire. Have a layer of chopped mushrooms stewed in butter in the dish, lay the cutlets on it, pour over some d'Uxelles sauce, and garnish with truffles, cut in very thin circles.

Mutton Cutlets à la Milanais.—Take six cutlets from a neck of mutton ("French chops," many butchers term them), mix equal quantities of grated Parmesan cheese and cracker meal. Dip the cutlets into rich thick brown sauce,† then into the cracker and Parmesan; shake off loose crumbs; dip them now into beaten egg in which a little salt and very finely chopped parsley and

---

* See No. II.   † See No. IV.

chives have been mixed, and then dip them a second time in the Parmesan and bread crumbs; drop them into a kettle of very hot fat; in four minutes they will be done. Do not fry more than four at a time, as too many cool the fat. Dish them in a circle with spaghetti dressed with Parmesan in the centre.

It seems to me just here that before giving further recipes for fried articles I had better make sure that all my readers understand the process of frying in deep fat. I have used the word *sauté* too, and although no doubt both these processes are familiar to most readers who would be likely to practise "Choice Cookery," for those who are not adepts many of the recipes would be impossible to execute. Frying, once understood, is so easy a process one wonders that so few should excel in it. To those who are not sure of themselves I recommend practice. A couple of hours' practice and careful observance of rules will enable a bright woman to fry successfully.

For this practice you may prepare several different articles and fry one after the other —one or two very soft and creamy croquettes, one or two breaded articles, especially such as are dipped in thick sauce before being crumbed, etc.

The principle on which articles that are very soft and creamy, underneath the surface of egg and crumbs, are fried is this : the creamy substances, whether rich sauce like d'Uxelles and Villeroi, or the cream used to mix croquettes, must always be made of stock that will jelly when cold. The sauce is used warm, and the articles are put to chill on ice, so that they are in a jellied condition. Now the fat into which they are plunged must be so hot that it sets the coating of egg and crumbs, which forms a thin shell, as it were, before the jelly has had time to melt; the shell once formed, the interior cooks in the intense heat very quickly. If the fat were not hot enough, croquettes would go all to pieces, and articles coated with sauce would lose the better part of it.

To fry, you require a stewpan or iron kettle; those called Scotch kettles are best, as they set into the range readily. A frying-pan is only useful for sautéing in little fat. Articles to be fried must be immersed in fat, and no frying-pan is deep enough to do this safely. Put two to three pounds of clarified dripping or lard into the kettle, and let it get very hot. This will be after it ceases to sputter—some time after, perhaps; but you must now begin to watch for smoke to rise from the *centre*. Have near you some little squares of bread crumb; drop one in from time to time; only when it colors *immediately* is the fat hot enough. At this point no time must be lost, and your frying begins.

Of course you will have the articles you intend to fry right at hand. You will also need a large dish, in which you lay common butcher's wrapping-paper (often called "kitchen paper") and a perforated skimmer —some like a frying-basket, and for very small things it is an assistance; but for croquettes, cutlets, etc., it is not necessary: they can be laid on the skimmer and dropped in the fat.

The easiest and safest way to fry is to use a cooking thermometer (pyrometers or frimometers they are sometimes called), and let the fat be 380° for croquettes, oysters, and articles that only require two minutes' cooking; 360° for cutlets and heavier articles.

The time required for articles to cook in the frying-kettle seems astonishingly short. For instance, a breaded chop will be cooked to a medium degree in two and a half minutes, well done in three minutes; but it must be remembered the heat is intense. Croquettes must never be left longer than two minutes, while whitebait (which, however, require special instruction to fry without getting them into a cake) need less than a

minute. Potatoes require longer than most
things; but the fat need not be cooler at
first, as would seem necessary, because they
are so full of water, even when well dried,
that they cool the fat rapidly.

Sautéing (a word that would be expressive
of the process in English would be a boon
to writers on cooking).—The process generally meant by "frying" is really sautéing;
yet so general has been the misconception
among all but professed cooks, that one has
to take the precaution in giving directions
for frying to say, "Fry *in deep* fat." It
ought to be understood that to fry is to *im-
merse* in hot fat. If some term suitable for
kitchen use could be found, half the difficulty would be over. In old English books a
very fair translation was used; they told
you to "toss the article in butter," but
though it rendered sauté "jump" fairly, it
did not express the process. There is neither
tossing nor jumping about it, unless an occa-
sional shake to the pan be called so; and as

"flat frying," "dry frying," are awkward, the sooner we boldly take sauté into common use, and let it become a kitchen word as familiar as fricassee (which surely must have been very unfamiliar once), the better.

To sauté—although every Bridget or Gretchen fancies she can do it—requires nicety and care to do it well, and is far more difficult than "frying in deep fat." The pan requires to be hot, also the fat or butter used, which should cover the bottom of the pan; a bright fire is required. Things that take long to cook require more fat than those that require but a short time. Effort must be made to adjust the proportion, as adding cold fat prevents browning. Veal cutlets and many other things are far better sautéd than fried. The articles sautéd require to be watched that they do not burn; yet they must not be too often turned, or they will not brown—except, of course, such things as are chopped, which require frequent stirring up.

In speaking of chilling articles coated with sauce to be fried, I omitted to give the caution that, in the case of meats, care must be taken not to leave them long enough to freeze the meat.

7

XI

ENTRÉES OF MUTTON CUTLETS OR CHOPS.

Mutton Cutlets à la Duchesse.— Take as
many cutlets (or French chops) as required.
Stew them in stock, with a small bouquet of
herbs, very gently until they are perfectly
tender. Take them up, skim the stock, and
strain it; return to a small saucepan, and reduce the liquid to a glaze; dip each cutlet in
the glaze and lay it aside. Have ready what
cooks now call a "panada," made of a gill of
thick white sauce, two yolks of eggs stirred
into it and allowed to approach the boiling-
point, but not to boil (this, of course, must be
done in a double boiler), or the eggs will curdle; chop a dessertspoonful of parsley very
fine; parboil and chop also very fine three
onions; pound thoroughly in a mortar eight
mushrooms; stir these all into the thick

sauce, with a saltspoonful of salt and a quarter one of pepper. Roll each cutlet in this force-meat (if found too stiff to adhere properly, moisten with a little cream or a little liquor from the mushrooms), lay them on a fire-proof dish, and cover with bread crumbs and bits of butter. Bake them until they are a golden brown. Serve with brown Soubise sauce.

Lamb Cutlets en Concombre. — Trim and cut six lamb cutlets three quarters of an inch thick, flatten them a little to make them of equal size and thickness; flour them, and sauté them in butter five minutes. The fire must be sharp, because they must be a nice brown on both sides. Arrange them round an entrée dish, with a gill of brown sauce poured outside, and a pint of fillets of cucumber in the centre.

To Prepare Fillets of Cucumber.—Cut firm fresh cucumbers lengthwise through the middle, remove seeds and all soft parts, cut into inch lengths and into olive shapes all the

same size. Put them into a stewpan with
an ounce of butter, a pinch of pepper, a saltspoonful of sugar and one of salt, and let
them stew until quite tender, without acquir-
ing any color. To do this the stewpan must
be closely covered and frequently shaken.

Lamb Cutlets with a Purée of Mushrooms.—
Trim and cook and serve the cutlets as in
the foregoing recipe, only in place of the cucumbers make a purée of mushrooms in the
following way: stew half a pint of button
mushrooms and part of their liquor in half
a pint of white sauce until they are very tender (taking care the sauce does not burn),
pound them in a mortar, then force them
through a vegetable strainer; then add
enough of the white sauce in which they
were stewed to make the purée the sub-
stance of very thick cream.

Cold Lamb Cutlets in Mint Jelly.—Roast a
piece of what butchers call the rack of lamb,
which is really the neck and ribs. Let it get
cold; cut from it six cutlets, which trim just

as if they were uncooked; that is to say, remove meat and fat from the bone, and scrape it. Mask each of the cutlets in mint jelly* warmed enough to be half fluid. Arrange very carefully round an entrée dish when they are perfectly set, so that the jelly will not come off. Have a Russian salad in the centre.

How to Prepare the Salad.—To prepare this you require two or three small vegetable cutters of pretty shape; use them to trim carrots, white turnips, and cucumbers into small, attractive forms; boil these in separate waters till tender; also green peas, sprays of cauliflower, and very tiny young string-beans. Throw each vegetable as it is cooked into ice-cold water to keep the color. Have some red beet-root boiled *before* it is cut into shapes. Use equal quantities of each vegetable. Arrange them with peas in the centre, and the others in circles round, studying the effect of color; then dress, but do not mask, them with green mayonnaise.

---

* For recipe, see No. V.

At seasons when materials for Russian salad cannot readily be obtained the chops may be served with a centre of cucumber salad, or one made of the small white leaves of lettuce.

Cutlets Chaudfroid à la Russe.—For this cold dish mutton cutlets are used. They must be of the finest quality, and from mutton not newly killed. Cut as many cutlets as required, trim, and scrape the bone. Braise for an hour in a moderate oven till the meat is very tender, remove, and press between two dishes until they are cold. Then trim each cutlet into perfect shape. Boil a quart of strong stock (which already jellies) down to less than half a pint; dip each chop into this glaze once or twice, till they look "varnished." You now require a pint of stiff aspic jelly; turn it out of the bowl, cut one or two slices a quarter of an inch thick from it, to be cut into shapes (or croûtons) with a cutter to garnish the cutlets. Chop the rest of the aspic, lay it round the dish, and the cutlets against it, with the croûtons ·of aspic to form the outer edge. The centre must be filled with a Russian salad, in this case stirred up with very thick mayonnaise, instead of being formally arranged. The mayonnaise must be only sufficient to dress the vegetables, none to run into the other materials, and beet-root must be added last, as it discolors the sauce if stirred up in it.

ENTRÉES OF SWEETBREADS.

Sweetbreads à la Suprême. — Take two plump sweetbreads, lay them an hour in strong salt and water, then boil them for ten minutes in fresh water; put them between two plates to flatten till cold. Cut off all the gristle and loose skin from underneath; put them to stew *very gently* in half a pint of good-flavored stock. Take them up, drain well, and stew them in half a pint of sauce suprême, with a dozen small mushrooms, for ten minutes.

Sweetbreads with Oysters. — Prepare the sweetbreads as in the foregoing recipe, quarter them, and put them in a stewpan with a gill of white stock, the strained liquor from two dozen oysters, a saltspoonful of salt, a pinch of pepper, and a suspicion of nutmeg. Put two ounces of butter in a stewpan over the fire, stir into it one tablespoonful of fine flour; let them bubble together, stirring the while, one minute. When the sweetbreads have been simmering twenty minutes, pour the gravy from them to the sauce; stir quickly till smooth. If thicker than very thick cream, add a little more stock. In five minutes add the oysters. Keep *at boiling-point*, but not boiling, till the oysters are firm and plump. Do not leave them in the sauce a minute beyond this, or they will begin to shrink. Take them and the sweetbreads up, and if the sauce is too thin to bear a wineglass of cream, boil it rapidly down till *very thick;* then skim, and just before pouring over the sweetbreads stir in a wineglass of thick cream. If it goes in earlier it may curdle.

It has been explained before, but I repeat it here, that there must never be too much sauce, however good, to any dish, and that the consistency is most important: it must be thick enough to mask a spoon, yet run from it freely. Nothing can be worse than a dab of white mush being served as sauce, unless it be a quantity of thin, milky soup floating on every plate. This is where the happy medium must be struck. It is perfectly easy to give exact proportions to produce certain degrees of thickness, and this has been done in the chapters on sauces; but where these sauces are used as a medium in which to cook, for instance, sweetbreads, a certain amount of liquid must be added to prevent burning. Now it is impossible to say how fast this added liquid will diminish if the simmering is as slow as it should be, it may lose hardly at all, in which case the articles stewed must be taken out, and a few minutes' hard boiling given to evaporate the liquid and bring the sauce back to the proper point.

Sweetbreads in Cases.—Prepare two sweetbreads as directed in the foregoing recipes. Put them in a stewpan with a thin slice of fat boiled ham, half a carrot, half a turnip, and a small onion, all cut small, and laid as a bed under the sweetbreads; put in a gill of broth, a bouquet of herbs, and half a salt-spoonful of salt, with a pinch of pepper. Let them stew, closely covered, one hour, turning them after the first half-hour. When done, take them up and drain them. When cold, cover with thick d'Uxelles sauce; sprinkle thickly with very fine bread crumbs. Make two rough paper cases, butter each liberally, and very carefully lay each sweetbread in one, crumbed side uppermost. Put them in a quick oven till pale brown. Have ready proper sweetbread cases, slip them neatly into them, and serve.

These are excellent cold, in which event they should not be shifted from the rough case until ready to serve.

XII.

ALTHOUGH these ever-popular dishes are all
or may all be prepared from one mixture,
there is a difference in the manner of using
it which I will here explain.

Croquettes are made from a soft creamy
mixture chilled on ice till firm enough to
mould, then simply dipped into egg and
crumbs and fried in very hot fat.

Cutlets are the same (of course fancy
cutlets are meant, not the French chops, so
called), only they are shaped to imitate a
real cutlet, with a little bone inserted; or, in
the case of lobster cutlets, a small claw is
used to simulate the chop bone. Many only
stick a sprig of parsley where the bone should
be, to keep up the fiction.

Kromeskies are rolls of the same mixture

enveloped in very thin slices (hardly thicker than paper) of fat larding pork; a small toothpick holds the pork in place. The rolls are then egged, crumbed, and fried.

Rissoles are the same thing, only rather easier to prepare, being rolled in very thin pastry instead of pork.

Cigarettes, the newest variation of the favorite entrée, and most dainty of them all in appearance, are thin rolls of croquette mixture (or, better still, quenelle meat) not thicker than a small cigar. These are rolled in pastry, thoroughly deadened, pinched very securely, and fried a very pale brown.

As the manner of making the mixture is about the same for all kinds of meats, fish, or game, varying only in flavor—a little wine, a little onion, or sweet herbs taking the place of the mushrooms in some cases— I will give exact directions for making sweetbread cutlets; chicken, game, or fish may be substituted for the sweetbreads, naming them accordingly. The ham may always be omitted where the flavor is objected to. For those who like it, it adds very much to sweetbreads, but would be out of place with game, which should depend on its own individual flavor.

Cutlets of Sweetbreads. — Soak a pair of sweetbreads in salt and water for an hour— longer if there is much blood about them; then cook them half an hour in stock. Drain them and let them get cold. Trim off all superfluous fat and gristle; chop them with one ounce of lean boiled ham to each pair of large sweetbreads, and half a can of mushrooms, a small teaspoonful of salt, the sixth of one of pepper. Put an ounce of flour in a small thick saucepan with an ounce of butter; stir them together over the fire until they bubble; then add a half-pint of liquid consisting of a gill of stiff jellied stock and a gill of thick cream; stir till they boil and form a smooth sauce; mix the sweetbread mixture with the sauce.

The mixture should be a soft, creamy mass, not in any way so stiff as sausage-meat, or so as to remain in a heap without spreading; when poured on a plate, it should be of a consistency that will *slowly* settle, yet there must not be any liquid whatever. On this question of consistency depends the quality of the croquettes, cutlets, etc., made from it. If too stiff, they will be dry and only a superior sort of hash ball. What you have to aim at is a croquette or cutlet that will ooze out of the thin shell of egg and crumb when pressed with a fork. Success in attaining this can always be secured by taking care to moisten the minced meat with a sauce made of *very stiff jelly* in the proportion of half a pint of liquid (the melted jelly and cream) and one ounce each of flour and butter. This will mix a pint of sweetbread and mushrooms, or rather less of dry meat, such as the breast of chicken, veal, etc.

I dwell on this point because this class of entrées is always popular, and if the consistency is once well understood, success is certain to follow.

When the mixture is poured into shallow dishes or plates, a piece of buttered paper should be laid over them, and then they should be placed on ice until quite firm. When ready, cut small pieces of the mixture, make them into shapes as nearly resembling a French chop as you can, using a very little cracker meal should they stick to your hands. Have before you a large dish of cracker meal and the yolks of two eggs beaten with two small tablespoonfuls of water, cover each cutlet thoroughly with egg, then with meal, gently patting them to make the meal adhere; insert anything you please to represent the bone (turkey ribs may be boiled white and kept for this purpose). Cutlets require to be dropped into very hot fat, and taken up within two minutes. Consult directions for frying in former chapter.

Sweetbread croquettes are simply made into cork or pear shapes, never large, instead of cutlets. When the white meat of chicken replaces half the sweetbread, they are called Cutlets, or Croquettes, à la Reine.

Make no attempt to mould croquettes or cutlets until the mixture is firm enough to cut; then handle very quickly, make into proper forms, finish them either as cutlets or what you wish, and let them remain in a cold place for an hour or two before cooking; this last direction may not be always possible, and to an expert is not necessary, but when time can be given the amateur should always plan to do it.

But though in experienced hands it is possible (though not so easy) to make croquettes and fry them as soon as breaded, do not be led to believe that you can dispense with putting the mixture on the ice the first time. I remember a young lady who was very proud of her croquettes telling me she never found it necessary to chill the mixture; she could secure perfect shape without. I asked to see the process, and decided in my own mind that she must go widely from the directions, and have her material as stiff as hash; but I found she solved the difficulty in a different way: she simply worked in quantities of cracker meal, using it like flour. Of course the croquettes were spoiled, although it was true they kept their shape, and I do not think the young lady realized at all that she was changing and impoverishing the preparation altogether.

Braised Sweetbreads. — Take a pair of sweetbreads, lay in salt and water for an hour, then blanch. Press slightly between two dishes; when cold, remove all skin, fat, and gristle; cut up very fine a small carrot, a turnip, and an onion; put them in a stewpan with the sweetbreads, pour over them a pint of stock, lay a piece of buttered paper over them, and braise carefully for half an hour. Take them out of the stewpan, put them in a small meat-pan, boil the liquor rapidly a couple of minutes, then baste the sweetbreads with it several times; put them in a quick oven to brown; serve on slices of fried bread, pour half a pint of Spanish sauce round, and garnish with mushrooms.

8

Tartlettes of Chicken.—Cut six ounces of the breast of a cooked chicken into very small pieces, chop up one truffle, twelve mushrooms, and two ounces of lean boiled ham; stir them into a gill of white sauce. Butter thickly nine dariole moulds, line them neatly with quenelle meat,* of which you will require half a pound, fill the centre carefully with the mixed chicken, cover the top carefully with quenelle meat, and steam for twenty minutes; dish on a circle of spinach, pour béchamel sauce over and round, fill the centre of the dish with peas or mixed vegetables.

Chicken à la Hollandaise.—Take out the breast-bone of a large *young* fowl, and fill the space with the following force-meat: half a pint of fine bread-crumbs, an ounce and a half of butter, a small boiled onion chopped, and a dozen oysters cut into small pieces; a saltspoonful of salt, a pinch of pepper; bind

---

. * See directions in No. IV.

together with an egg, sew up the fowl, and truss for roasting. Make a nice batter, as for fine fritters, and when the fowl has been in the oven half an hour, pour part of the batter over it; when dry and beginning to brown, pour more, until it is thickly coated and a nice brown; baste often; cut up the chicken, and serve with Allemande sauce and lemon.

XIII.

THE directions for making one kind will serve for patties generally. In cities the cases are very easily bought, but where they have to be made at home, only one who is already an expert in making puff-paste should attempt them.

Patties when served as an entrée should be quite small, or half of them will certainly be left on the plates.

Roll puff-paste a quarter of an inch thick for each patty, cut three circles from it, moisten the surface of two very slightly with water, place one on the other, then with a sharp penknife cut a circle nearly through the third round, leaving a margin of one third of an inch; lay this round carefully on the other two; brush the top with white of egg (be sure not to touch the sides), and bake in a very quick oven. Patties must be watched, and turned if they show signs of rising unevenly. When they are a fine yellow-brown take them out, and leave five minutes for them to cool slightly, then with a penknife or a boning-knife carefully remove the top formed by the smaller circle you marked, and which (if the paste was very light and the oven in good condition) will probably have risen out of the centre. Be careful in handling these covers, for while warm they are very brittle. With a coffee-spoon remove the hàlf-cooked dough from the centre of the patty, taking care, however, to leave sufficient thickness of inner crust to prevent the sauce from oozing through.

The filling for patties can be made before it is needed; but when that is done, it must be made quite hot before it is put into the cases, as, if it were put in cold, the pastry would burn before the inside became warm.

Dresden Patty Cases.—These make a very
pretty kind of patty when puff-paste is not
to be had, and even when it is are a desirable variety.   They are made from fine light
baker's bread.   Cut slices an inch and a half
thick, then with a biscuit cutter about two
inches in diameter cut circles from these
slices, and with another cutter, a size smaller,
press half-way through each.   You will now
have pieces of bread the size and shape of
patties.   Beat four eggs; mix with a pint
of milk and a saltspoonful of salt; pour this
into a shallow pan, and stand the bread patties in it.   The amount of milk and eggs
must of course depend on the number of
patties; the proportion named is enough for
six small ones.   The patties must remain
steeping until they are thoroughly soaked;
they must be carefully turned upside down
when the lower part is sufficiently steeped.
The time required will depend on the quality
of the bread, but one hour will generally
suffice.   The bread must be thoroughly pen- .

etrated by the custard, be almost as moist as mush, yet be in no danger (with careful handling) of breaking. When sufficiently steeped, take each one on a cake turner and lay it on a drainer. (They may be prepared some hours before they are needed for cooking.) When quite drained, baste each one carefully with beaten egg till every part is coated, then smother it in cracker meal. Gently pat it to make it adhere, then slip the patty on to a dish till you are ready to fry. Do not attempt to move the patties with the hand or a spoon, but with a flat skimmer or cake turner.

When prepared as directed, make three pounds of lard *very hot* in a deep frying-kettle,* place three of the patties on a fine wire frying-basket, and fry brown. The fat should be excessively hot, as the patties, being full of cold custard, will not burn, and will rapidly cool it. They should be a delicate brown

---

* See full directions for frying in No. X.

in six or seven minutes. Let the fat come back to the original intense heat before putting in the other patties. When they are fried, remove the centre you marked with the smaller cutter with a sharp thin knife and small teaspoon, leaving the sides about half an inch thick. They are now ready to fill. If the patties are just right, the inside you remove should be of a custard-like texture, *not* like sopped bread : indeed, in eating them, the bread should not be easily detected. These patties are very delicious filled with any of the usual fillings, or, for dessert, with stiff preserve. They have no covers, consequently the filling should be piled high without allowing the sauce to run over, and garnished with parsley or water-cress.

Sweetbread Patties.—Soak two very white sweetbreads in salt and water one hour ; parboil for twenty minutes ; then let them cool ; remove the skin, fat, and gristle ; cut them into half-inch dice, and lay them aside while you prepare the following sauce : Put a gill

of strong white stock into a small saucepan
with a gill of mushroom liquor (and a dozen
small mushrooms cut in four if approved) to
boil. In another saucepan cook an ounce of
flour and one of butter together, stirring till
they bubble; pour the two gills of stock
quickly to it, and stir till smooth. Season
with half a teaspoonful of salt and very little pepper; lay in the sweetbreads, and let
them stew twenty minutes. Strain them off
from the sauce, which boil down (stirring
constantly to prevent burning) till very thick;
then add a gill of thick fresh cream. The
sauce should now be thick enough to mask
the spoon *very heavily;* pour it over the
sweetbreads, and stir together. This is now
ready for filling the patties. If mushrooms
are not liked they may be omitted, the liquor replaced by a gill of stock and a teaspoonful of white wine.

Oyster Patties.—Take a dozen and a half
Blue Points, scald them in their own liquor,
but do not leave them a moment after they

reach the boiling-point; strain the liquor from them; cut each oyster in four. Put a tablespoonful of flour and one of butter into a small saucepan over the fire, stir them together until they bubble; then pour to them half a pint of the strained liquor of the oysters, or part liquor and part stock. Stir continually, and let the sauce boil very thick; then lay in the oysters, and simmer half a minute. The amount of seasoning required will depend on the saltness of the oysters, but a saltspoonful of salt will probably not be too much, a little pepper, and a teaspoonful of essence of anchovies—just enough to make the sauce a delicate salmon-color. For the last thing, stir in one small teaspoonful of lemon juice. The consistency of the sauce for all patties should be that of very thick double cream. When it is not thick enough, it can always be reduced by boiling down, taking care not to boil the meat or oysters, etc., in it.

Chicken Patties.—Take the breast of a

boiled chicken, cut it into dice; use half a pint of the liquor in which it was boiled to make the sauce. Put this broth in a small saucepan with a teaspoonful of lean boiled ham chopped a little (take care there is not a particle of the outside of the ham, or it may impart a smoky flavor); let the ham simmer in the broth while you melt together a table-spoonful of flour and one of butter; when they bubble, and the broth has been boiled down to about one half, *strain* the latter into a half-pint measure, fill up with cream, and stir this quickly to the flour and butter. When the sauce is thick and smooth, put in the chicken; keep the mixture at boiling-point five minutes, then set the saucepan in another of boiling water, and stir in the beaten yolks of two eggs; only just let them thicken; then remove from the fire, and use for filling the patty cases. A teaspoonful of sherry is often added to the sauce. If this filling is not used while hot, it must be re-heated in a double boiler and watched, or the eggs will curdle; or the filling may be prepared and the eggs added after it is reheated.

Bouchées of any kind are simply patties made very small indeed—for this reason the filling is always *chopped* instead of being cut into dice.

The essence of anchovy mentioned is a most useful sauce for fish, and can be bought at any large grocery.

XIV.

In an earlier chapter I gave directions for quenelles as an adjunct to soups and for garnishing. Used in this way, they are only a revival of an old French fashion, coarsely imitated in the benighted days of Anglo-Saxon cookery by the English "force-meat balls." Lately, however, not only are quenelles a great feature in high-class cookery as additions to made dishes, but they are a most fashionable and delicious entrée, and replace with great advantage the too-frequent croquette.

To prepare quenelle meat for entrées.

Mode No. 1.—To make quenelle meat, a mortar is indispensable, as it must be pounded to a pulp that will go through a sieve, and I have known a persevering woman grate the breast of chicken on a large grater, but this is very slow work. Take the white meat from a large, young, uncooked chicken, and remove all skin, fat, and sinew. Melt together over the fire a scant tablespoonful of butter and one of flour; when they are thick and smooth, stir in a gill of boiling water quickly. This should now be a thick paste; put it away to cool. Take half as much butter as you have of chicken, and half the quantity of paste (technically called panada) that you have of butter. Put the paste into a mortar; pound it well; add the butter; pound again till smooth; add the chicken, cut up very small, and pound until the whole forms a smooth pulp. Add one whole egg and the yolks of three, the third of a salt-spoonful of white pepper (salt must depend on whether the butter seasons sufficiently). Work all well together, stir in half a gill of thick cream, and pass the whole through a wire sieve. Put the whole on ice to get firm. The quenelles should be about the size of a small egg flattened; shape with two tablespoons dipped in flour. Have ready a frying-pan with boiling water in which is a saltspoonful of salt, lay each quenelle carefully in, and poach for ten minutes. The water must boil very gently. Drain on a sieve; serve with mushroom or tomato sauce. Have a little dried parsley and grated tongue or ham, and scatter alternately on each quenelle.

Mode No. 2.—One pound of lean veal cutlet; pound it thoroughly in a mortar; then rub it through a sieve, or it may be forced (*after* it is pounded) through a vegetable strainer. Steep a pound of bread crumb in tepid water; wring it in a cloth to get rid of the moisture; put it in a stewpan with a tablespoonful of butter and a pinch of salt. Stir it over the fire until it ceases to stick to the pan and forms a smooth paste. Place it between two plates to cool. This is called bread panada. Put into a mortar twelve ounces of the prepared veal, six ounces of fresh butter, and eight ounces of the panada. Pound all well together; mix in gradually one whole egg, two tablespoonfuls of thick cream, and the yolks of four more eggs, a scant teaspoonful of salt, and a quarter-salt-spoonful of pepper. When this is all pounded into a smooth, compact mass, put it into a bowl and place it on ice until required for use. Mould and poach as described in last recipe.

Great care is required in cooking quenelles, as if they are overdone they become tough; ten minutes is enough for those the size of a small egg. Before moulding the whole, poach a small one, break it open, and ascertain if it is smooth, light, yet firm. They should melt in the mouth. If they are at all tough, add a little more cream to the mixture, unless the toughness comes from over-boiling, which you must guard against. Very elaborate quenelles are made with a core of dark meat, made by chopping up ham, tongue, or truffles very fine, and insert-

ing it in the centre while forming the quenelles. Always serve quenelles with tomato,
mushroom, or rich Spanish sauce. Dish in
a circle, and fill the centre with spinach,
green peas, or a macédoine of mixed vegetables.

The mode of preparing all quenelles is by
one of the two methods just given, but they
may be made of any kind of game, or the
backs of hares or rabbits. Quenelles of salmon, lobster, or other fish must of course be
served with appropriate fish sauce.

Timbale of Chicken à la Champenois.—
Chop a small slice of lean boiled ham, weighing about two ounces, put into a saucepan
with four chopped mushrooms, four truffles,
and an ounce of butter; stir in a moderate
dessertspoonful of corn-starch and half a
pint of stock and a gill of sherry; let this
slowly simmer until reduced to one half.
Skim off the fat, then stir in the finely
chopped breast of a large chicken or of
two small ones, six small pickled gherkins,

9

a sprig of parsley, and six anchovies which have been soaked in milk. Make all hot over a slow fire, but do not let them boil. Line a mould with light puff-paste, pour the mixture into it, and bake one hour; turn out and serve very hot. Garnish with fried parsley.

Scallops of Chicken à la Périgord.—This dish may conveniently be made when the white meat of chicken is required for other purposes.

Bone the legs of two large chickens; take half a pound of veal, a quarter of a pound of fat salt pork; pound both in a mortar, then pass through a sieve; add to this two table-spoonfuls of minced tongue, six truffles, and half a dozen button mushrooms, the yolks of two eggs, a saltspoonful of salt, and a *very little* cayenne. Mix well. Stuff the legs of the fowls with this. Sewing them up neatly, wrap each up in buttered paper; put them in a stewpan with two ounces of butter and a carrot, turnip, and small onion cut

up; add three quarters of a pint of brown
stock. Put the stewpan in the oven, baste
well, and cook gently one hour. When
cooked, have ready a mound of spinach.
Take a *very sharp* knife, cut the legs in
slices so as to make circles like slices of sausage; strain off the gravy. Cook together
a dessertspoonful of butter and flour; when
they bubble, pour the strained gravy to it,
with a gill of sherry and a little salt and
pepper; stir till smooth; boil till as thick as
cream. Dress the scallops of chicken in a
circle round the spinach, pour the sauce
round all, and insert bits of truffle and of
tongue between the scallops.

Chicken Soufflé.—Pound three ounces of
the white meat of cooked chicken as fine as
possible; mix with it half a pint of cream
and three well beaten eggs, a few button
mushrooms finely chopped, a saltspoonful
of salt, a sixth of one of pepper, a dust of
cayenne, and a speck of powdered mace. Pour
the mixture in a well-buttered mould, tie

a cloth over it, and steam it half an hour. It must stand quite upright in the steamer. Turn out on a hot dish, and pour any rich brown sauce preferred around it. This soufflé may be made of sweetbreads, or half and half. If individual soufflés are preferred, butter as many dariole moulds as the mixture will fill; lay at the bottom of each something by way of garnish—a little star or disk of tongue or ham for some, of truffle for others, of green gherkin for others— so that when turned out the top of the soufflés will show spots of color. Half fill the moulds, and steam twenty minutes.

Soufflés of all kinds depend for excellence on being served the moment they are ready, and on the steam being kept up all the time they are cooking. When baked the oven must be very steady.

Fritot of Chicken.—Take a cold chicken, cut it into small neat joints, season rather highly with salt and pepper, strew over them a small grated onion (or one very finely chopped), and a dessertspoonful of chopped parsley. Cover them with oil, and then squeeze over them the juice of a lemon. Turn the pieces now and then, and let them remain until they have absorbed the flavor. Meanwhile make a batter of four table-spoonfuls of flour and about eight of milk, or as much as will make a thick smooth batter; stir into it a wineglass of brandy and an egg, the whole beaten to a high froth. Leave this batter in a warm place an hour before using, dip the pieces of chicken into it, and fry in very hot, deep fat. Serve piled high on a dish garnished with fried parsley.

XV

Cigarettes à la Reine.—These are the newest development of the rissole and croquette. They require strict attention to details to secure perfect form. Roll puff-paste a quarter of an inch thick; prick it all over—this is to deaden it; roll it now till it is no thicker than cartridge-paper. Cut it with a sharp knife dipped in flour into strips about two inches and a half wide and about the length of a cigar; lay on each strip a roll of chicken quenelle meat that is very firm, and the roll not thicker than a lady's slender forefinger; be careful that the meat reaches nearly the whole length of the paste, yet leaves a margin for closing, as the least oozing will spoil the appearance. Moisten the edges of the paste all round with white of egg; fold the paste over half an inch; be very careful to see that it adheres thoroughly; then pinch the ends. Roll them gently with a cool hand on the floured board to round them without pressure, taper off the ends cigar fashion. If they are softening, lay them on a floured plate on ice to get firm; then roll them in egg and very finely sifted cracker meal. You may roll or improve the shape, if there is any irregularity, while crumbing them. Remember what you aim to imitate is a cigar. The great danger for the first time is getting them too large; they must therefore be very slender. Fry in deep fat just as rissoles; serve on a napkin, log-house fashion. These dainties, as will have been seen, have a large amount of butter, and soften in a warm room; they must therefore be made in a cold room, and if set on ice some hours before cooking will be much easier to fry without bending or twisting.

Cigarettes à la Chasseur are, as the name indicates, made of game, in exactly the same way as the last recipe.

Lobster Quenelles.—Prepare with bread panada as directed for quenelle meat. Poach
and drain them. Then dish in a circle with
thick Hollandaise sauce in the centre and
round them.

Chicken, Turtle Fashion.—This requires a
pullet or young hen about six months old.
Bone the bird; stuff with a force-meat made
of four parts minced veal, two parts chopped
hard eggs, a half part lean boiled ham, two
parts mushrooms, and two parts *pâté de foie
gras.* First make the veal and ham hot in
a little butter, then add the mushrooms and
foie gras; moisten with stock or mushroom
liquor, and *gently simmer* five minutes. Stir
in two beaten yolks of eggs and a teaspoonful of lemon juice. Season with a saltspoonful of salt, a quarter one of white pepper,
and a tiny pinch of nutmeg, grated. Stuff
the fowl with this mixture; sew it up with
trussing-needle and string; turn the skin of
the neck half over the head, and cut off part
of the comb, which gives the appearance of

the turtle's head. Scald and skin four chickens' feet; cut off the claws, and insert two where the wings ought to be and two in the thighs, so as to look like turtles' feet. Put in a stewpan a tablespoonful of chopped boiled ham, an onion, and a small carrot cut up, with a tablespoonful of butter; let them brown very slightly, add half a pint of stock, skim it, lay the fowl in this stock, and stew gently for an hour and a half to two hours, or even longer, according to size. When quite tender take up the fowl, cut and remove the string with which it is sewn, lay it on its back on a dish, garnish the breast with sliced truffles cut in fancy shapes, place a crawfish tail to represent the turtle's tail. When eaten hot serve velouté sauce. This is an excellent dish cold garnished with aspic.

Baked Ravioli.—Four ounces of veal, six ounces of butter, three ounces of lean sausage-meat, a teaspoonful of mixed sweet herbs, a little salt and pepper. Pound all in a mortar; when smooth, pound separately a gill of spinach that has been boiled till just tender without losing color, and a quarter of a pound of cream cheese or rich cottage cheese, which must be squeezed in a cloth to remove all the milk. When smooth, pound all together, and stir in the yolks of two eggs. Make some pastry with half a pound of butter, three quarters of a pound of flour, and the yolks of two eggs; mix stiff, and roll till about as thick as a fifty-cent piece. Cut the paste in two parts. Take a medium-sized biscuit-cutter, mark half as many circles on one half the paste as you wish ravioli. Lay in the centre of each circle a mound of the force-meat — perhaps a large teaspoonful, only be careful to leave a quarter-inch margin all round. Moisten this margin with a camel's-hair brush dipped in white of egg; lay the second half of the pastry over these mounds; press the cutter on each to trim them, and you have a number of little round patties; press the edges together very well by curving the little finger round them. Have some rich stock boiling in a stewpan; poach the ravioli five minutes. Take them up, drain them well, arrange them in a fire-proof gratin dish, sprinkle them over with grated Parmesan cheese, pour in a very little stock, and bake brown in the oven.

Veal Cutlets à la Primrose.—Take a pound of veal cutlet; cut it up into small cutlets the size of a dollar, and perfectly round. Put two ounces of butter (which has been first melted to let the curd separate) into a saucepan, with three onions, two ounces of bacon cut into small dice, a bouquet of herbs (including bay-leaf). Fry, stirring frequently, for a quarter of an hour, then add a tablespoonful of corn-starch, a dessertspoonful of Tarragon vinegar, and a pint of strong stock. Let all simmer very gently for about one hour. Take up the cutlets, strain the gravy and pour it over them, then sprinkle with a tablespoonful of grated tongue, and the same quantity of parsley dried and crumbled small. Chicken may also be cooked in this way.

Quails à la Lucullus.—This, as its name implies, is a most expensive and luxurious way of serving these dainty birds, yet by management the livers of chickens may be saved a day or two by scalding them, and the opportunity taken when several are required for general use during a week. Bone very carefully six or eight quails. Cut up three ounces of unsmoked bacon, put it in a sauté pan, let it cook five minutes, then add the livers, a shallot sliced, a small bouquet, twelve white peppercorns, six cloves, a salt-spoonful of salt. Let all cook carefully ten minutes: nothing must burn or get very brown. When cooked, pound well in a mortar, pass through a sieve, then add three truffles chopped; stuff each quail into shape, butter some paper cases known as "quail cases," put a quail into each case, a few drops of olive oil on each breast. Then put them in a quick oven for ten minutes or a quarter of an hour. For the gravy, put the bones of the quails in a stewpan, add a tablespoonful of glaze and a gill of brown sauce, with one tablespoonful of water. Simmer till the gravy is well flavored from the bones, then strain, and add two tablespoonfuls of chopped truffles and half a gill of sherry. Put one tablespoonful of this sauce over each quail before sending it to the table, after very carefully draining all grease from the quails. These are served in the papers, but rough paper cases may be made to bake them in, and the regular crimped ones set in the oven to get hot just before dishing up. Slip the quails into them after draining.

Quails à la Jubilee.—Bone as many birds as required. Lard them with pork and thin strips of truffles. Stuff them in shape with equal parts of sweetbreads and oysters, sew them up; roll them in buttered paper, and cook in the oven in enough Chablis to cover them. Pound some boiled potatoes and water-cresses together until thoroughly blended; put a tablespoonful of butter in a saucepan with one of milk; put in the potato, stir round till quite hot; use this to make a border on which to serve the quails. When they have cooked fifteen to twenty minutes, take them up, glaze them (melt glaze in a cup standing in hot water, and brush them over). Lay them on the potato border, and pour into the centre some Spanish sauce with mushrooms in which has been boiled a slice of lemon.

XVI.

Pigeon Cutlets.—Take half a dozen young pigeons, split them down the back, and bone them, all but the leg, cutting off the wings at the second joint. Cut each bird in two down the breast; trim off all ragged edges, so that each half-bird has as much as possible the appearance of a cutlet, the leg serving for the bone. Sauté these cutlets, having seasoned them with pepper and salt, for three minutes in hot butter, then put them in the oven for five minutes. When done, press between two plates till cold. Then mask each cutlet with a thick purée of tomatoes and mushrooms in which aspic jelly has been mixed, equal parts of each. Let them be put on ice to stiffen the masking. Roll in fine cracker meal, then dip into well-beaten egg, again into the meal, and then place them in a sauté pan with very hot clarified butter, and cook them a fine golden brown. Dish up on a border of mashed potatoes browned with grated Parmesan; serve mushrooms in the centre and Spanish sauce all round.

Pigeons à la Tartare.—The pigeons should be trussed for broiling; flatten well with a rolling-pin without breaking the skin, season them with pepper and salt, dip into clarified butter and cover with very fine crumbs or cracker meal. Broil them carefully, turning often. Make a sauce of a scant tablespoonful of finely chopped parsley, a shallot, two spoonfuls of pickled gherkins, and a boned anchovy. Mince all finely and separately. Squeeze over them the juice of a lemon; add half a tablespoonful of water and six of oil, and a little pepper. Mix all very well, and just before serving rub in a teaspoonful of dry mustard. Put the sauce into the dish, lay the pigeons over, and serve.

Compote of Pigeons. — For any dish of pigeons except roast or broiled, wild birds may be used in place of tame. Their flavor is far finer, and if not perfectly young, which is the main objection to the use of wild birds, the preparation remedies the defect. Cut four ounces of lean unsmoked bacon into pieces, and fry five minutes. Split the pigeons in half, skewer each half as neatly as possible with tiny skewers, so that they will not sprawl when dished; flour and season them lightly, and fry a nice brown on both sides; add one small carrot, one small turnip, two sticks of celery, one shallot, six mushrooms—all cut small; add a *bouquet garni* and three gills of rich stock; let them all simmer very slowly in a stewpan for one hour, or longer if the birds are not young. Simmer together a tablespoonful of flour and one of butter; pepper and salt (quantities depend on whether the stock be seasoned); stir constantly, and when they begin to change color pour a gill of brown stock

- 10

to it, stirring well; remove from the fire. Take up the pigeons, strain the gravy, then stir in the brown thickening you have made; boil up, skim off all fat, then return the birds; let them get thoroughly hot, but not boil. Serve on a border of mashed potatoes, pour the gravy round and over them, and fill the centre with peas or spinach.

Soufflé of Partridges.—Clean and cook two partridges; remove the breasts and best of the other flesh without skin or sinew. Take two ounces of rice cooked till very tender, pound them together in a mortar with one ounce of butter and a gill and a half of glaze melted, a teaspoonful of salt, and a sixth of pepper. Pound until the whole can be forced through a strainer, then add the beaten yolks of four eggs, and last of all the whites of two beaten till they will not slip from the dish; stir them very lightly into the mixture. Pour it into a silver soufflé case, or into a number of the small china cases. Bake till it rises, and then serve immediately with a tureen of rich brown sauce. This soufflé can be made of any kind of cold bird or fish. The four eggs are given for *medium*-sized partridges.

Salmis of Snipe.—Clean and roast lightly six snipe, saving the trail. When done let them get cold, then cut them up and remove the skin, and lay them in a buttered stewpan; pound the trimmings and bones in a mortar, and put them into a stewpan with two shallots, a clove, a bouquet of herbs, and half a pint of claret; let this simmer until reduced to one half. Then add three quarters of a pint of Spanish sauce. Let these *very gently simmer* for half an hour, skimming frequently; strain through a fine sieve, and return to the stewpan. If it is not thick enough to coat the spoon, reduce a little more. Pour this sauce over the snipe in the sauté pan, and let it get hot without boiling; pile the pieces in a pyramid; meanwhile chop the trail, mix with half the quantity of *pâté de foie gras* and a little salt and pepper;

spread this on croûtons, bake, and use them to garnish the snipe.

Fillets of Teal with Anchovies.—Remove the breasts from a pair of teal after they have been three parts roasted. Take care to preserve each half breast in good shape. Lay these fillets seasoned in a china fire-proof dish which has been well buttered and strewed with grated Parmesan; split two anchovies, remove the bone. Wash and dry the four halves, lay one on each fillet of teal, moisten with a gill of fish stock, sprinkle with bread crumbs and grated Parmesan cheese, lay small pieces of butter over, and bake in the oven fifteen minutes. The last thing before serving squeeze the juice of a lemon over all.

Rabbits are so little cared for in this country that it may seem useless to give recipes for using them. There are probably two reasons for the low estimate in which rabbit is held here. One, that as they are offered in market they are skinny, miserable animals.

Yet there are parts of the country where they attain a good size, and a fine plump rabbit may compare favorably with fowl for many purposes. Indeed, English epicures use it in preference for mulligatawny. The second reason, and probably the one that is the real reason, for the difference in taste is because, being so lightly esteemed, no care is ever given to the preparation of them.

On the chance that some reader may feel inclined to test the possibilities of the native rabbit, and its claims to a place in choice cookery, I give two or three recipes, each admirable in its way. Rabbits should be used quite fresh, and cleaned and wiped dry as soon after they are killed as possible.

Grenadines of Rabbit à la Soubise.—Take the whole backs of two rabbits from the shoulders to the thighs, both of which you reject; cut away the ribs and the thin part that forms the stomach, leaving only the backbone with solid flesh each side; divide this into sections, about two joints to each.

Lard them, and then braise for one hour. Stand them in a circle, and pour over and round them a pint of brown Soubise sauce.

Fillets of Rabbit with Cucumber.—Half roast a rabbit, then remove the solid flesh from each side the backbone in long fillets. Cut two cucumbers and one Bermuda onion in thin slices, salt them, and let them drain. Lard the fillets of rabbit, season them, and lay them in a stewpan, with a pint of white sauce slightly thinned with white stock, the cucumber, and the onion. Let them simmer for half an hour. Lay the fillets in a circle, and put the cucumber and onion in the centre, the sauce, which should be thick enough to mask them, over the fillets. Fried sippets garnish this dish.

A Civet.—For this dish the dark-fleshed rabbit, or hare, as it is often called, is best. Cut it into meat joints; cut half a pound of unsmoked bacon into slices, and fry in a saucepan; then lay in the hare, and sauté for fifteen minutes. Pour off the fat. Add half a pint of port-wine, a bouquet garni, and a dozen mushrooms, and a little pepper and salt; let this simmer gently one hour; then add a pint of brown sauce and twenty button onions which have been blanched. Simmer for another half-hour. Remove the bouquet, add a gill of stewed and strained tomato, half a gill of glaze, and a tablespoonful of Chutney. Serve in a pyramid, pour the gravy, after it is well skimmed, over the whole, and garnish with fried croûtons.

Timbales d'Épinard.—Make some quenelle meat of chicken or veal according to directions already given, and mix with purée of spinach, prepared as follows, until it is a nice green; pick and wash some spinach, put it into salted boiling water, and boil fast for fifteen minutes. Drain and press it, then beat it through a wire sieve; return to the saucepan with two ounces of butter; pepper and salt; stir till well mixed. Stir a gill of cream to the quenelle meat, then use enough of the spinach to give it a fine light-green color. When well mixed, butter some dariole moulds; nearly fill them. Then dip your finger in cold water and press a hole in the centre of each to the bottom; fill it with a purée of ham, and then put a coating of quenelle meat over, and steam twenty minutes.

Purée of ham is prepared as follows: pound lean boiled ham in a mortar with some stock that has been boiled down to half glaze; rub through a wire sieve. If too stiff, moisten with a little more melted glaze.

XVII.

COLD ENTRÉES, OR CHAUDFROIDS.

THESE elegant dishes are suitable for formal breakfasts, luncheons, and suppers, and while presenting an unusually attractive appearance, are easier to manage than less elaborate dishes, because they can usually be prepared, all but garnishing, the day before.

Although in giving the recipes meat cooked for the purpose will always be directed, and for formal purposes no care or expense should be spared, the intelligent reader will see where she may make a very pretty dish by utilizing cold fowl, game, or lamb for any simple occasion.

Sweetbreads au Montpellier.—Parboil a pair of fine white sweetbreads, after soaking them in salt and water an hour. Let them get cold between two plates under slight pressure.

Cut them into the form of cutlets (cutlet cutters are to be obtained at the fashionable New York hardware stores, and at the large French tin-shops down-town). Have some firm aspic jelly not quite set; dip each cutlet in it; chop some aspic that is hard and cold roughly; form a circle of it; arrange the cutlets on this; fill the centre with asparagus heads; pour mayonnaise round, and garnish with fancy shapes of aspic, red and white alternately. Red aspic is colored with pulp of the red beet stirred into it while liquid and then strained out; green is produced by spinach. The various shades of amber, shading into rich brown, that are so effective when tastefully mingled, are due to caramel coloring. When colored aspic is required for garnishing, pour off a little into separate vessels, and color each as required.

Chicken Salad à la Prince.—Cut the white meat of cold fowl into neat fillets, using a very sharp knife, so that there may be no ragged edges. Mask each piece with a mixture made as follows : One tablespoonful of finely minced capers, two of minced boiled ham, three hard-boiled eggs, an anchovy boned and washed, and two sardines freed from skin.   All these must be well pounded, then rubbed through a sieve ; add a teaspoonful of finely minced tarragon and chives. Stir all into a tablespoonful of mayonnaise and one of aspic, semi-fluid of course.   When each fillet has been well coated with the mixture and has set, line a border mould with aspic jelly, ornament the fillets of chicken with little strips of beet-root and cucumber arranged like a trellis-work.   Place them very carefully round the mould on the layer of aspic, then pour in a little more aspic, until the border mould is full, and set it on ice.   When about to serve have a dish well layered with the small leaves of lettuce. Drop the mould for one minute in warm water, and turn out on to the lettuce.   Fill the centre with a salad composed of cucumber cut into dice, peas, string-beans cooked until tender (for this purpose the canned French string-beans serve admirably, being beautifully cut ready). Pour over the centre salad some thick mayonnaise.

Where mayonnaise makes too rich a dish for the digestion, béchamel sauce may be substituted for masking, but never for salad; for instance, two very simple chaudfroids of chicken may be made as follows:

Chaudfroid of Chicken, No. 1.—Cut up a young fleshy chicken into neat joints, remove the skin, mask each piece carefully with béchamel sauce; when quite set arrange on chopped aspic in a circle, garnish with strips of cucumber and beet; cut the remainder of the cucumber and beet into neat pieces, and stir into a gill of mayonnaise, and use for the centre. This and all salads should be lightly seasoned before the mayonnaise is added, or they are apt to taste flat.

Chaudfroid of Chicken, No. 2.—Prepare the chicken as in last recipe, only before masking the joints season the béchamel well with finely chopped tarragon; leave out the mayonnaise and aspic. Pile up the pieces of chicken on the entrée dish, and garnish with Roman lettuce, or, if that is not to be had, the hearts of Boston lettuce.

Chicken and Ham Cutlets.—Boil a young fowl with a good breast in clear stock; take it out, let it get cold; cut the breast into rather thin slices. The bones, skin, and trimmings may be thrown back in the stock, which can be boiled down to make both the béchamel and aspic for the dish (see recipes), or be kept for other purposes. Take the slices of chicken and some very well cooked lean ham that is cut so thin you can see the knife under the slices. Melt a little béchamel sauce, that must be like blanc-mange, pour it on a plate, and before it has time to cool cover the plate with the slices of chicken. Dip the ham into the stock (if it has been boiled down to jelly, otherwise into melted aspic), lay the ham over the chicken, then more thin slices of chicken. Now cover the whole by means of a spoon with more béchamel; when all this sets, which, as your sauce has only been half melted, it will do quickly, you have a large white cake about half an inch thick. Cut this cake into small pieces (unless you have a cutlet cutter), as like a cutlet in form as possible, using a sharp penknife or boning-knife. Take up each carefully, and with the end of a silver knife or small spoon cover the edges with the béchamel sauce, which must be nearly set for this purpose.

To garnish the cutlets, cut some tiny green leaves from pickled gherkins, and red ones from the skin of a red pepper-pod, and place two of each in the centre of each cutlet, star-shaped; a touch of white sauce will make them stick; place a speck of parsley not larger than a pin's head in the centre. Stick a tiny lobster claw three quarters of an inch long at the narrow end of the cutlet, and place them in a silver dish round some aspic of a bright amber color, chopped. Put a very small sprig of parsley between each cutlet.

I may here remind the reader that when aspic or béchamel is used for masking or for pouring into a mould as lining, etc., it must *not be made hot*, only softened in a bowl set in warm water, just enough to be free from lumps. It must, of course, be stirred from the moment it begins to soften. The mould to be lined should be turned about till it is well coated, and if there is a disposition to run off the sides, roll it round in ice. For instance, when the first layer of béchamel is poured on the plate as directed in last recipe, it must be moved about until quite covered, yet very thinly. If it sets too soon, hold the bottom of the plate over steam.

Reed-birds in Aspic.—Take the back and breast bone from a dozen birds, splitting them down the back first. Save the feet. Make a force-meat of *pâté de foie gras* and panada in equal proportions; season highly, spread the inside of the birds, sew them up

as nearly in shape as possible; bake seven
to ten minutes, then dip them into glaze;
put a little paie aspic in a dozen dariole
moulds, enough to cover the bottom a quarter of an inch, and when just set put in a
bird breast down; set on ice a few minutes,
then pour in aspic to cover the bird a quarter
of an inch. Put on ice. Turn out, and on
the top of each strew pistachio nuts chopped
very fine. Insert the two feet of the bird,
scalded and dried, to stand up from the
centre.

Chaudfroid of Reed-birds.—Prepare as in
last recipe with *pâte de foie gras* force-meat.
Butter a dozen dariole moulds. Put a bird
in each, breast downward; put the dariole
moulds in a pan with a little water, and set
it in the oven for fifteen minutes; when cold,
turn out the birds, wipe them, dip each in
brown *chaudfroid* sauce, and put them on a
dish to cool. When cold, lay them in rows
against a pile of chopped aspic.

Brown Chaudfroid Sauce is made by putting a pint of Spanish sauce, a gill of cream, half a pint of aspic jelly together, and boiling them until they are reduced one quarter. Skim constantly, and strain for use.

White Chaudfroid Sauce is simply béchamel and aspic treated in the same way. It differs, of course, from plain béchamel in having the piquant flavor of the aspic; in appearance there is little difference.

11

XVIII

Iced Savory Soufflé. — This dish can be made of fish, game, or chicken, but is considered best made of crab. Cut up the crab, or whatever it may be, into small pieces; let it soak in mayonnaise sauce for two or three hours. Have some well-flavored aspic jelly, half liquid; whip it till it is very frothy; put some of this at the bottom of the dish it is to be served in—a silver one is most effective; then place a layer of crab well seasoned, and fill it up with aspic and crab alternately until the dish is nearly full; place a band of stiff paper round, and fill in with whipped aspic; set it on ice for two hours; take off the paper, and serve.

Savories.—Within the last few years, which may, perhaps, be called the renaissance of cooking in England, since Kettner, in his "Book of the Table," shows that in the Middle Ages that country was famous for its cuisine, while France was still benighted—within the last few years, then, there has grown up a fashion of introducing preparations called *savories*. They vary very much, from the tiny little *bouchette* of something very piquant, to be taken between courses as an appetizer—which, I believe, was the original idea—to quite important dishes suitable as entrées for formal breakfasts or suppers. But it is with the original "savory" as a piquant mouthful that they will take their place in this book. So important a part have they come to play in English *menus* (I am not now speaking of simple dinners) that the invention of a new "savory" is something to be proud of, and it is said that the very best are invented by the *bons vivants* themselves, seldom by the *chef*. One lady has written a book of which *savories* is the only branch of cooking treated, and she says in her preface, " Savories being at present so fashionable, and novelties in them so eagerly inquired for, I have been induced to publish a small book on the subject."

In looking over any list of small savories we find many of our old friends in it, such as *cheese canapés, angels on horseback, anchovy toast*, etc. With these familiar dainties we will have nothing to do, only the mention of them will serve to show that any little piquant morsel may be used as an appetizer served as *hors d'œuvres*.

The Savage Club Canapés.—These must be made small enough not to require dividing— in other words, can be eaten at one mouthful. Cut slices of stale Vienna bread a quarter of an inch thick, stamp out from them with a very small cutter circles about the size of a fifty-cent piece. Sauté these in a little hot butter till they are a very pale brown. Lay them on paper when done, to absorb grease. Stone as many small olives as you have guests; fillet half as many small

anchovies—that is to say, split them, and remove the bones and scales; wash them, dry
them, and roll each one up as small as possible, and insert it in an olive in place of the
stone.   Now trim one end of the olive so that
it will stand; then put a drop of thick mayonnaise on the centre of one of the rounds of
fried bread, which, of course, must be quite
cold; stand the stuffed olive on it neatly, and
put one drop of mayonnaise on the top, to
cover the opening in the olive.   A variation,
and I think an improvement, on this bouchée,
is to use a little softened aspic to attach the
olive, and a small quantity finely chopped to
crown it.   Still another plan is to put a tiny
disk of bright-red beet on the top, using aspic to cement it there.

Canapés à la Bismarck.—Cut circles with
a small cutter from slices of stale bread a
quarter of an inch thick; sauté in butter till
they are a light brown; spread over each
when cold a thin layer of anchovy butter;
curl round on each an anchovy well washed,

boned, and trimmed; sprinkle very finely shred olives over them. Anchovy butter is two parts butter and one of anchovy paste.

Caviary Canapés.—Cut some slices of bread a quarter of an inch thick; cut disks from them with a small round cutter; fry them pale brown in butter. When about to use them chop a large handful of water-cress leaves very fine, taking care to press them in a cloth to remove all water before you begin to chop; when they are almost as fine as pulp, mix with them an equal amount of butter; when well blended, spread each canapé with it, and spread a layer of caviare on the top.

Prawns en Surprise.—Cut some small rounds of bread and butter, not more than two inches in diameter and a quarter inch thick. Peel some prawns; steep them in mayonnaise sauce a few minutes; place three on each round of bread-and-butter, with a small piece of water-cress on each. Place over all some whipped aspic jelly; strew lobster coral over them.

Prince of Wales Canapés.—Take some fine prawns, three anchovies, two gherkins, and two truffles. Bone the anchovies and wash them, peel the prawns, and then cut all the ingredients into very small dice. Make a sauce as follows: Bruise a hard-boiled yolk of egg in a mortar with a tablespoonful of salad oil, a saltspoonful of mustard; mix with this an anchovy and a teaspoonful of tarragon that has been scalded and chopped; pound all well together, and pass through a sieve with a teaspoonful of tarragon vinegar and a speck of cayenne; mix enough of this with the prawns, etc., to season the mixture. Salt, it will be observed, is not mentioned, because the anchovies and prawns may be salt, but this can only be known to the cook by tasting. Butter some small water biscuits (crackers), put a small teaspoonful of the mixture on each, and cover with finely chopped aspic. Garnish by putting a spot of green gherkin on one, a spot of red beet on another, and on a third one of truffle, and so on alternately.

Shrimp Canapés. — Fry some rounds of bread as directed for other canapés. Make some shrimp butter by pounding equal quantities of shrimps, from which heads, tails, and shells have been removed, and fresh butter till they form a smooth mass; spread the fried bread with it. Place whole shrimps on the top in the shape of a rosette, in the centre of which put a tiny pinch of chopped parsley.

Cheese Biscuits à la St. James. — Take three tablespoonfuls of the finest flour, half a pound of cream curds, and five ounces of Brie cheese, which has been carefully scraped, and a pinch of salt; pound all in a mortar; add five ounces of softened butter and three eggs, to make a very stiff paste, which must be rolled very thin, and cut into round biscuits. Bake in a very quick oven, and serve hot.

Kluskis of Cream Cheese. — Take half a pound of fresh butter, six eggs, six tablespoonfuls of cream cheese, a pinch of powdered sugar, salt, and sufficient grated bread crumbs to make a paste, adding cream if it crumbles; mix well together, and roll into small balls; poach them in boiling water until firm (no longer). Serve hot, with a spoonful of poivrade sauce on each.

Cold Cheese Soufflés.—Grate one and a half ounces of Gruyère cheese; the same of Parmesan. Whip half a pint of cream and a gill of aspic jelly to a high froth; stir in the cheese; season with salt, cayenne, and made mustard to taste. Fill little paper baskets or very small ramequin cases, grate cheese over the top, and set on ice to get firm.

The above mixture may be frozen just as you would ice-cream, but very firm, then cut out in little cubes, and serve on canapés of fried bread; it is then called "Croûtes de Fromage Glacé."

Oysters à la St. George.—Take the beards from two dozen oysters; put the melt (or soft roe) of two Yarmouth bloaters into a sauté pan with two ounces of butter; dry and flour the oysters, and sauté them with the melt. Have some squares of bread fried a nice light brown; place a nice piece of the melt on each square, and an oyster on top; squeeze a few drops of lemon juice on each, and serve very hot.

Allumettes.—For these fantastic little trifles you require anchovies preserved in oil—not in salt; they are found at all Italian groceries and at the larger American grocers'. Wipe them free from scales and oil; cut each into long, thin strips. Have ready some plain pastry rolled very thin; envelop each strip of anchovy in pastry; pinch closely, so that it will not burst open, and fry in very hot fat for a half-minute, or sauté them in butter till crisp and yellow. Serve log-house fashion, using two allumettes for each crossing instead of one; put fried parsley in the corners, and serve very hot.

Eggs à la St. James.—Take as many eggs as you have guests, and boil them hard in buttered dariole moulds; the moulds must be large enough to hold the egg when broken into it, but not much larger. When quite cold remove the eggs; slice off the white at one end of each, taking care to preserve the shape. Scoop out the yolk; mix this with a teaspoonful of chopped truffles, a little pepper and salt, and put it back very neatly into the whites. Coat the eggs with aspic jelly several times. Serve them upside down, that is, the uncut part upward. Put a spoonful of half-mayonnaise (mayonnaise mixed with whipped cream) on each, and a few specks of chopped truffle.

A variety of this dish has anchovy paste in very small quantity in place of truffle, and the mayonnaise just made pink with it.

XIX.

GALANTINES are so useful and handsome a dish in a large family, or one where many visitors are received, that it is well worth while to learn the art of boning birds in order to achieve them. Nor, if the amateur cook is satisfied with the unambitious mode of boning hereafter to be described, need the achievement be very difficult.

Experts bone a bird whole without breaking the skin, but to accomplish it much practice is required; and even where it is desirable to preserve the shape of the bird, as when it is to be braised, or roasted and glazed for serving cold, it can be managed with care if boned the easier way. However, if nice white milk-fed veal can be obtained, a very excellent galantine may be made from it, and to my mind to be preferred to fowl, because, as a matter of fact, when boned there is such a thin sheet of meat that it but serves as a covering for the force-meat (very often sausage-meat), and although it makes a savory and handsome dish, it really is only glorified sausage-meat, much easier to produce in some other way.   This is, of course, not the case with turkey ; but a boned turkey is so large a dish that a private family might find it too much except for special occasions.   On the other hand, galantines of game, although the birds may be still smaller, are so full of flavor that it overwhelms that of the dressing.

The following process of boning, however, applies to all birds.   To accomplish the work with ease and success, a French boning-knife is desirable, but in the absence of one a sharp-pointed case-knife may do.   Place the bird before you, breast down, with the head towards you.   Cut a straight line down the back through skin and flesh to the bone.   Release with the left thumb and forefinger the skin and flesh on the left side nearest to you, and with the right hand keep cutting away the flesh from the bone, pulling it away clear as it is cut with the left hand. When you reach the wing joint cut it clean away, leaving the bone in the wing, and continue cutting with the knife close to the bone until all the meat from the left breast is released. Return to the back and continue to separate the meat from the bone, always keeping the edge of the knife pressed close to the latter, until the leg is reached; twist it round, which will en-able you to get the skin over it, and cut the joint from the body bone. Proceed with the right side in the same way, using your left hand for cutting and your right to free the meat (to some this would be very awkward, and when it is so turn the bird round). The bird will now be clear of the carcass. Lay the bird flat on the board, inside upward, then cut out the wing-bone and proceed to the legs; cut the meat on the inside of each thigh down to the bone and clear the meat

from it, cutting it each side until you can lift
the bone out; then free the drumstick in the
same way.

If it be intended to stuff the bird in form,
it would be necessary to bone the leg and
wings from the inside, but for a galantine it
is useless trouble, as they are to be drawn inside the bird. Spread out the bird, having
drawn legs and wings inside, season with a
teaspoonful of salt and half a saltspoonful of
white pepper mixed together, and rubbed
over the flesh, which must have been made
as even as possible by cutting the thick parts
and spreading them over the thin ones. If
there are any bits of meat clinging to the
bones they must be carefully gathered together and chopped with a pound of veal and
two ounces of lean cold boiled ham, with four
ounces of fat, sweet, salt pork. (Butter may
be substituted if pork is objected to). When
all is chopped as fine as sausage-meat, season
rather highly with pepper and salt. Spread
a layer an inch thick over the bird; then

add some long strips of tongue, some black truffles cut into dice half an inch square, and a few pistachio nuts. Dispose these, which may be called the ornamental adjuncts of the galantine, judiciously, so that when cut cold they will be well distributed. Cover carefully with another layer of force-meat, fold both sides over so that the force-meat will be well enclosed, form it into a bolster-shaped roll, tie it up in a linen cloth securely with string at each end, and sew the cloth evenly along the middle, so that the shape will keep even. Put it into a stewpan with stock enough to cover it, two onions, two carrots sliced, a stick of celery, a small bunch of parsley, a dozen peppercorns, an ounce of salt, and the bones of the bird, well cracked. Let it *simmer gently* for three hours and a half. Take it up, strain the liquor, and let the galantine get nearly cold. Take off the cloth; wring it quite dry; put it on again, rolling the galantine as tight as possible; tie firmly, and place it on a platter;

cover with another platter, and place a heavy weight upon it to press it into shape. Let the stock get cold. Take off the grease. Add a half-teaspoonful of sugar and the juice of a quarter of a lemon to the stock, and reduce by rapid boiling to a half-glaze, that is to say, a jelly firm enough to cut into forms without being tough. Clear with white of egg in the usual way, and when quite transparent pour part into shallow dishes, leaving enough to cover the galantine. Color one dish a rich clear brown; leave the rest light. When the jelly thickens, but is not quite set, cover the galantine with it half an inch thick. When the jelly is cold, cut it into what are called *croûtons*, which may mean vandyked strips, to be laid across, triangles, squares, or any fancy shapes; the pieces and trimmings are chopped to scatter over the dish or lay in small piles round.

Ballotines are small galantines made by treating small birds as directed in last recipe, only that the force-meat should have a larger

12

proportion of truffles, and be made of the same kind of bird; for instance, grouse would have rich force-meat of grouse. One grouse, however, would make two or four ballotines; quails make two, to be served as individuals.

Galantine of Breast of Veal. — Bone a breast of young white veal very carefully, spread it out as flat as possible on the board, pare the meat at the ends for about an inch so that the skin may project beyond. Take all the scraps of meat that may have come from boning, provided they are not sinewy; take also twelve ounces of veal cutlet, and half the quantity of fat unsmoked bacon. Chop very fine, seasoning all rather highly. When the meat is fine, season the inside of the veal. Mix with the force-meat tongue, truffles, and pistachio-nuts or olives, all cut into half-inch dice (the tongue larger). So mix these that they will come at regular intervals through the stuffing. Roll the breast round the stuffing, which is not spread, but laid in a mass, and sew the veal together.

Fasten it up in a cloth, tie securely at the ends, then tie bands of tape round at intervals to keep it in shape.

Braise this galantine for six hours in stock, which may be made of a small knuckle of veal and the bones and trimmings. Vegetables as directed for chicken galantine.

Let the galantine be cold before it is untied. Garnish and glaze as directed for chicken.

Galantine is occasionally made of sucking pig, and is very popular in France. The pig must be carefully boned, all but the head and feet. A sufficient quantity of veal, of fat unsmoked bacon, and of bread panada must be chopped and pounded to make enough forcemeat to stuff the pig in the proportion of one part bacon, two panada, and three of veal, seasoned with a teaspoonful of onion juice and two of powdered sage.

The pig's liver must have been boiled in stock, and cut in dice. There must be fillets or strips of rabbit or chicken, a few chopped truffles and olives. Mix well. Lay in the fillets as you stuff the pig, and when full sew up the opening. Try to keep the shape as near as possible. Then braise slowly for four to five hours, as directed for galantine of veal. Do not remove the cloth till it is cold.

XX.

I HAVE spoken several times of "filleting." To some readers an explanation of the term may be necessary. To "cut up" a bird does not indicate the meaning, nor does the term "to carve" it do so, because to carve means to cut up or divide with an exact observance of joints and "cuts." Filleting, when applied to anything without bones, as the breast of a bird or boned fish, means to cut into very neat strips that are thicker than slices; but when you are directed to "fillet" a grouse or a chicken, it is intended that you should cut it into small neat portions regardless of joints and without the least mangling of it; therefore a very sharp knife must be used, and either a small sharp cleaver or a large cook's knife only to be employed when a bone has to be cut through.

To Fillet Cooked Birds: Grouse, Pheasants, or Poultry.—Cut the bird in half straight down the middle of the breast-bone, using a large sharp knife for the purpose. Lay each half on the table and take out the breast-bone from either side. If the bird is a large fowl, duck, or partridge, each breast will make three fillets, and leave a good piece with the wing, but average birds only make two breast fillets. Chop off the pinions within an inch of the meat, then cut the wing in two neatly; drumsticks are to be chopped off close to the meat, and divided into two fillets (if a large chicken or duck; leave game whole); cut the thigh in two also. Trim very neatly; leave no hanging skin; indeed, when filleting for *chaudfroids* the skin should be entirely re-moved, and both it and the leg-bones are re-moved for pies. When possible, it is better not to use the drumsticks. From a chicken they make an admirable "devil," and from game they help the bones and trimmings to make a rich gravy ; so it is no waste to discard them.

Cold pies are of two kinds : the one cooked in a terrine or dish without pastry ; the other in what the English call a "raised paste," and the French a *pâte chaude.* Those with paste—which is seldom eaten—are far handsomer, but do not keep so well—that is to say, they must be eaten within three or four days even in winter; while in a terrine carefully kept in a cool airy place the pie will be good at the end of three weeks.

On the other hand, the pie in a terrine is much less trouble to make. Proceed as follows :

Game Pie.—Make some force-meat thus : Fry a quarter of a pound of fat ham cut in dice with half a pound of lean veal. Take the ham up before it gets brown, as you do not need it crisp; when the veal is cooked take that up also, and if there is enough of the ham fat in the pan, put in half a pound of calf's liver cut up in dice, if not, sauté it in butter. In sautéing all these they must be often stirred, as you want them well cooked and yet not very brown. When done they must be finely chopped, then pounded in a mortar, with a small teaspoonful of salt, and half a saltspoonful of pepper. Then add a dozen mushrooms chopped, and mix the whole.

A game pie is usually made rather large, and the greater variety of game used, the better; partridge, pheasant, grouse, hare, all help one another, but at least two kinds are necessary. It must be boned and neatly fil-leted into small joints. Put on all the bones and trimmings to stew in three pints of wa-ter, with a good-sized carrot, onion, a stick of celery, a small bouquet, a clove, a tea-spoonful of sugar, one of salt, and a little pepper; boil all this until the bones look white and dry when out of the stock. Strain, and reduce by rapid boiling to a half-glaze; put a layer of the force-meat at the bottom of the dish, then one of boned game, with a sprinkling of pepper and salt, and either a little finely chopped parsley or, what is far better, a few thin slices of truffles; pour over a little of the reduced stock; fill the dish in this way to within an inch of the top; make a plain flour-and-water paste, lay it on the pie, and make a hole in the centre, bake slowly in a pan of hot water. When cold, remove the paste, cover the top with chopped aspic, fold a napkin, and serve the terrine on it, with a wreath of parsley round the base. Game pie is not a dish to be eaten at one or even two meals (unless very small), therefore the aspic must be fresh each time it is served.

French Method of Making a Game Pie or Pâte Chaude.—Make a paste of two pounds of flour and one of lard or butter, with salt to taste and about half a pint of water; knead it into a smooth, rather hard paste; put it into a damp napkin for an hour. Butter a raised pie dish—a tin one that opens to release the pie—line it with the paste rolled half an inch thick, letting it come half an inch above the dish; line the inside of the paste with buttered paper, bottom and sides, and fill with rice or corn meal; cover with another piece of buttered paper, wet the top of the pastry all round, and lay a cover of thin pastry over it; trim very neatly, make a hole in the centre, and ornament with leaves cut from the paste and laid on; the under side should be slightly moistened to make them adhere. Brush the surface with well-beaten egg, and bake about an hour, when it should be a nice golden brown. Take off the cover; after it has slightly cooled, remove the rice or meal and the buttered paper; take the case from the mould, and brush it all over with egg inside and out; set it in the oven until the glazing dries, and any part that may not be sufficiently brown becomes the color of the cover, which, being glazed at first, is not returned to the oven.

Preparation for Filling the Case. — Fillet

chickens, guinea-hens, partridges, or grouse (leave pigeons or quails whole, but bone them). Put sufficient pieces of one sort, or all sorts mixed, to fill the pâte chaude case into a sauté pan, with two ounces of butter, and sauté till lightly colored. Take them out, and put them in a stewpan with a quart of reduced consommé, half a pint of mushrooms sliced, a dozen truffles cut into dice (half-inch), a teaspoonful of salt, a little pepper, and a wineglass of sherry, and let them simmer very gently, *not boil*, for half an hour, or until very tender. Let them cool, and when lukewarm arrange them in the pâte case, leaving the centre hollow, which fill with mushrooms and truffles. The liquor in which they were stewed must be then poured over them. The cover of a pâte chaude case is often not used, and aspic jelly covers the top of the pie.

English Manner of Making Game Pie in a Crust.—Use at least two kinds of game, which for this purpose must not be long kept;

high game is acceptable to epicures when roasted or stewed, but never in a pie. Discard all parts blackened by shot. Cut into neat joints, from which bones must be removed. Take all the fragments from the carcass after the breast and joints are removed, and the flesh of a small bird or hare, or, failing that, some calf's liver fried in dice; pound whichever you may have for forcemeat in a mortar with four ounces of bacon that has been boiled; when the whole forms a paste (from which you have removed all strings, sinew, or gristle while pounding), season with pepper and salt—a teaspoonful of salt to a pound of force-meat, and a scant half saltspoonful of pepper. Put on the bones, *without vegetables*, in cold water to simmer until it is a rich broth, which strain, and boil rapidly till a little set on ice in a saucer will jelly. Make what is called "raised" paste in the following way: To two pounds of flour use three quarters of a pound of butter and half a pint of scalding milk; pour this into a hole in the centre of the flour, and knead into a firm paste, adding a little more milk if necessary (but it seldom is). This paste is not to be rolled, but beaten out with the hand while warm to half an inch thickness. Line a well-buttered meat-pie mould, with a hinge opening at the side; leave half an inch of paste above the mould; trim off neatly with scissors. Then lay in the game and force-meat in alternate layers, seasoning the joints with pepper and salt as you lay them. A few slices of tongue and truffles to form one layer are desirable. When the mould is full, lay on the cover, moisten the under edge, and pinch round in tiny scallops. Make a hole in the centre, round which put an ornament; stick in a bone to prevent the hole closing, and bake two to four hours in a moderate oven, according to size, remembering always that the crust will not be injured by long baking, and that the game in this pie is uncooked. When it is removed from the oven, let it stand half an hour, taking the mould off, that it may cool; then brush the sides and top with an egg beaten with milk, and return the pie to the oven that the sides may brown; cover the top, if it is already highly colored, with a sheet of paper. Remove the bone from the centre, insert a small funnel, and after removing all fat from it, pour in the gravy from the bones. The gravy must be poured very slowly or it will bubble up, and care must be taken to have all the pie will hold, yet not a drop too much, or it will ooze somewhere. These pies, when quite cold, may be sent any distance, and are much used in England and Scotland for hunting-parties, besides being a standard breakfast and luncheon dish. The crust is merely a frame to hold the game.

XXI.

In all choice cookery the appearance of dishes has to be carefully studied. However good the taste may be, the effect will be spoiled if its appearance on the table does not come up to the expectation raised by the name on the *menu*. For this reason the subject of garnishes requires to be considered apart from the dishes they adorn. In the old time garnishes were few and simple, and when not simple, very ugly, as the camellias cut from turnips and stained with beet juice. Nowadays garnishes are many, and many so termed form part of the dish, as what are termed, "floating garnishes for soup," quenelles, etc. Garnishes that are merely ornamental need not be so expensively made as those intended for eating. Foremost among

fashionable floating garnishes for soup are
the colored custards known as pâte royale;
they are perfectly easy to make, yet very effective served in clear bouillon.

Colored Custard. — Prepare the custard
with five yolks of eggs, a gill of cream or
strong bouillon, and a pinch of salt; butter
small saucers or cups; divide the custard in
three—color one with spinach juice or pulp
of green asparagus, another with red tomato
pulp or the pulp of red carrot boiled, and a
third with pulp of beets. A few drops of cochineal may be added to intensify the color
of the last, which is apt to be a beautiful
pink instead of red. The custard for which
pulps are used must be strained after they
are added, expressing as much of the juice as
possible. The custard should be flavored
delicately with the vegetable used for color.

Spinach Juice is very frequently directed
to be used as coloring, but scarcely anywhere
is any indication given that the juice without
preparation is of very little use. It should

be prepared as follows : Take a large handful of fresh green spinach, wash it, and remove decayed leaves only; drain well, then
pound in a mortar or chopping-bowl until
quite mashed. Let it stand a quarter of an
hour, then squeeze the mass in a cloth, and
put the green water into a cup, which set
over the fire in a small saucepan of water;
watch the scum rise ; when it stands quite
thick at the top and turns a vivid green, remove at once (if it remains on the fire after
this the green darkens); pour the contents
of the cup through cheese-cloth or thin muslin laid in a strainer. The scum that remains is your coloring matter. It must be
carefully scraped off with a spoon, and mix
with the custard only as much as is required
to give a delicate green tint. If any is left
it may be mixed with an equal quantity of
salt and put away; it loses color, however,
after a few days.

The colored custards must be set in water,
a small piece of buttered paper over each,

13

and the water allowed to boil gently round them till they are firm. Let them get quite cold; then cut them into cubes or diamonds.

Profiterolles.—Perhaps the next in popularity of these floating garnishes are *profiterolles*, or " prophet's rolls," as cooks call them. They are made exactly like those intended for dessert, omitting sweetening of course, and a very small quantity is required, as they must be dropped no larger than a pea, and baked a *pale* fawn-color.

Put a gill of water and a pinch of salt and two ounces of butter in a small saucepan; as soon as they begin to boil draw the saucepan back and stir in four ounces of flour; beat well over the fire with a wooden spoon until it becomes a soft paste, then add the yolks of two eggs and white of one, beating each yolk in separately. It will be seen that the paste is similar to that made for cream cakes.

A similar garnish is made in the following way: Beat an egg with a pinch of salt, and then stir in as much dry sifted flour as the egg will moisten; work it well with the hands till it is elastic, although stiff. Roll it on a pastry board until it is as thin as paper, then roll it on a clean linen cloth still thin- · ner, and leave it a quarter of an hour to dry. Then fold the paste, press it very tightly together, and with a tin cylinder, not larger in diameter than a cent, cut out, with consid- erable pressure, as many small disks as you require to allow five or six to each plate of soup. Have ready in a small saucepan some *smoking hot* lard. Drop the disks in; they will puff and swell till they are like marbles. Stir them, and take them out of the fat; they require only a few seconds to brown, and must be taken out very pale. Add to the soup the last thing before serving.

While aspic jelly is certainly the hand- somest of garnishes for cold dishes, it is gen- erally part of the food itself, and should not be so lavishly used that when helped there is more jelly than meat served. Where the jelly is intended only for a garnish not to be eaten, simple gelatine is sufficient. For instance, a large platter containing a galantine or a *chaudfroid* may have a handsome wreath glued on the border, of red and green leaves, or holly leaves and red berries, or any device that need not be disturbed by the carver.

For such decorations as these gelatine is melted in proportion of three ounces to a scant quart of water, cleared with white of egg, and then colored pale yellow with caramel or saffron, vivid red with cochineal, and bright green with spinach; it saves time and trouble to let this congeal on dishes in thin sheets. Small cutters of ivy, oak, and other leaves can readily be purchased at the large house-furnishing stores.

One word here about uneatable decorations, never admit them at a children's party; they are the very part of the feast the little people will most crave; red leaves for them must be of red currant-jelly, yellow of white, etc.

"Forced butter" is another form of garnish which adds much to the appearance of
glazed ham or tongue. It is butter beaten
to a white cream, then put in a forcer, and a
pattern traced on the ham, which must be
followed just as in icing a cake.

A Few Ways of Cooking Vegetables.—It is
not intended to go into the general cooking
of vegetables, although it may be said that
even the choicest cooking can offer no greater luxury, or, alas! a greater rarity, than a
dish of early peas or asparagus *perfectly
cooked*. But this is not the place to remedy
the wholesale spoiling of summer vegetables
that goes on in almost every kitchen. I will
only give what may be a few new ways of
preparing familiar vegetables.

Stuffed Artichokes.—Wash the artichokes;
boil till nearly tender; drain them; remove
the middle leaves and "chokes" (this is the
fibrous part round the base); lay in each a
little rich force-meat, and put them in the
oven to cook until the meat is done. Serve
with rich brown gravy.

Fried Artichokes. — Cut in slices length-wise; remove the chokes, cut off the tops of the leaves, wash them in vinegar and water, drain them, and dip them in frying batter. Fry in very hot oil or lard. Serve with fried parsley sprinkled with salt.

Beet-root Fritters. — Cut boiled beets in slices; slice raw onions; scald them; dry them well; then lay one slice of onion, sprinkled with chopped chervil, pepper, and salt, between two slices of beet. Dip them carefully in frying batter, and plunge into boiling fat; when pale brown take them up.

Cauliflower Fritters. — Parboil the cauli-flower—that is to say, boil until it begins to be tender—about fifteen minutes; then plunge it into ice-cold water; this keeps it white. Break it up into branches. Dip each one into thick béchamel sauce slightly warmed; let them get cold; then take each piece separately and dip it into carefully made fry-ing batter, and drop them into boiling lard; fry a pale brown, and serve garnished with fried parsley.

XXII.

VARIOUS WAYS OF SERVING VEGETABLES.

Stuffed Cucumbers.—Cut large-sized young cucumbers into slices about two inches thick, rejecting the ends. Peel, and remove the seeds; scald the slices for ten minutes, plunge them into cold water, and drain them. Line a fire-proof china dish with very thin slices of unsmoked bacon which has been scalded; make some veal force-meat such as directed for galantines; fill the holes in the centre of the rings of cucumber till it is level with the surface on both sides; wrap each up in a slice of bacon broad enough to cover it. Tie round with a string, pour a pint of strong stock into the dish, and bake twenty minutes in a slow oven. When done, take up the cucumber, drain, and remove the bacon carefully so as not to disturb the stuffing. Lay in a dish, and serve with Robert sauce.

In the following recipes the mushrooms to be used are the large flap ones. When canned ones will serve, the fact will be stated.

Mushrooms Stuffed à la Lucullus.—Wash, dry, and trim large mushrooms; chop up the stalks and broken ones fine with a teaspoonful of minced parsley, pepper, salt, and a tomato; make these hot in a tablespoonful of butter. Fill the mushrooms with the mixture, place them on a buttered baking-dish, and bake six minutes, basting them once or twice with clarified butter.

Mushrooms and Tomatoes.—Toast some slices of bread, cut them into rounds two inches in diameter, and butter them. Peel some firm tomatoes, cut them into thick slices, and lay them on the toast. On the top of each place a peeled mushroom. Put them on a dish that can go to table, pour a little clarified butter over them, put them in a hot oven for three minutes, and baste well. Serve hot and quickly.

Mushroom Jelly.—Take two pounds of

mushrooms, put them in a stewpan over the fire with a gill of strong consommé. Squeeze in a few drops of lemon juice, add a little pepper and salt, unless the consommé was salt enough. Melt in a gill of water half an ounce of gelatine, and strain it. When the mushrooms are quite soft, pass them through a sieve, mixed with the gelatine, and pour the mixture into a mould which has been rinsed with water. When set, turn out and garnish with finely chopped aspic, and a few cherry tomatoes if in season.

Mushroom Baskets. — Make some puff-paste; roll it out *very* thin. Line some small suitably shaped moulds (darioles will do very nicely); fill the centre with uncooked rice or flour to keep the shape while baking; cut some strips of paste, twist them, and bend them into the shape of handles; bake them very pale. When the pastry cases are done, empty out the rice, remove them from the moulds, and fill with the following mixture: chop as many canned mushrooms as you require with a small shallot, squeeze to them the juice and pulp of a large tomato, and put them in a stewpan with a tablespoonful of butter and a tablespoonful of very thick white sauce. Stir till about the consistency to eat with a fork. Squeeze a few drops of lemon juice over the top. Put the handles in so that they stand over the tops. Decorate with fried parsley.

The large Spanish or Portuguese onion that has of late years appeared in the markets is not often properly cooked. It is the most delicate and delicious of all onions, lacking the usual intense heat and rank odor. For this reason persons who wish to eat onions, either for health or inclination, will find this large onion cut up with ordinary salad dressing a great improvement even on Bermudas. This onion is full of a milky juice, which is lost in cooking if it is cut. Therefore, where a simple dish is required, the best way is to boil it, without peeling or trimming, for three hours if it weighs three pounds (it must be tender right through); then take it up, strip it, and remove the root, stalk, etc. Pour over it a rich white sauce, and serve, taking care that the gravy that runs from the onion is served with it. A still better way when an oven is not wanted is to bake them. Put them in a dripping-pan in the oven without removing peel or stalk. Bake at least four hours in a moderate oven. It will burn and blacken outside, which is of no consequence. Keep it turned so that the darkening may not go deeper one side than the other. When quite tender (but do not try it until it begins to shrink, or you will let out the juices), so that a knitting-needle will run through it, take it out of the oven, strip off three or four skins, remove root and stalk, and place the onion, without breaking it, on a dish; put a piece of butter as large as an egg, with a salt-spoonful of salt and a quarter one of pepper worked in it, on the onion; cover it, and put in the oven till the butter melts, and serve very hot.

Stuffed Spanish Onion.—Parboil a Spanish onion; then drop it into ice-water; take out the centre and fill it with force-meat; cover with a thin slice of sweet fat pork; sprinkle with a teaspoonful of salt and the same of sugar; add four tablespoonfuls of stock, cover closely, and cook over a good fire. When the onion is tender, take it up, remove the pork, strain and skim the gravy, pour it over, and serve. The best force-meat for the stuffing is made of cold chicken, a shred of boiled ham, a little chopped parsley, half a dozen mushrooms, all chopped well and mixed with a tablespoonful of butter and pepper and salt.

Potatoes à la Provençale.—Mash and pass through a wire sieve two pounds of potatoes; season with pepper and salt. Grate two ounces of Gruyère (Swiss) cheese, pound it with enough butter to make a paste, add a gill of milk and a teaspoonful of chopped parsley; put this in a sauté pan, add the potato, mix all well, and stir until the mass is pale brown; serve as a pyramid.

Milanese Potatoes.—Bake large potatoes till just tender; cut off the tops, which keep. Scoop out the potatoes, but do not break the skin. Mash the inside with butter, pepper, salt, and grated Parmesan; about a teaspoonful of butter and cheese to each will be the right proportion. Beat the potato mixture with a fork for a minute to make it light, refill the skins, put on the covers, and heat them in the oven.

Scalloped Potatoes.—Mash two pounds of potatoes with milk, and pass through a sieve; add three ounces of butter melted, two ounces of grated Parmesan cheese, and a little pepper and salt. Fill shells with this mixture, and brown them in the oven. Glaze them over with butter melted and grated Parmesan; return one minute to the hottest part of the oven. Serve very hot.

Tomato Jelly.—Two pounds of tomatoes, half a grain of red pepper, and two small shallots. Place them in a stewpan and boil till quite soft. Melt half an ounce of gelatine in as little white stock as possible; add this to the tomatoes, and strain; if not perfectly clear, clarify with white of egg in the usual way. Mould, and serve with chopped aspic round it. A little grated Parmesan may be sometimes sprinkled over it for a change.

Tomato Soufflé. — Prepare some tomato pulp, taking care to boil it down if too liquid; stir in the yolks of three eggs, then the whites well beaten; salt to taste. Fill either a large soufflé case or several small ones. Bake in a hot oven till it rises very high and is set in the centre; serve instantly.

Spinach Fritters.—Boil the spinach till it is quite tender; drain, press, and mince it fine; add half the quantity of grated stale bread, one grate of nutmeg, and a *small* teaspoonful of sugar; add a gill of cream and as many eggs as will make a batter, beating the whites separately; pepper and salt to taste. Drop a little from a spoon into boiling lard; if it separates, add a little more crumb of bread; when they rise to the surface of the fat they are done. Drain them, and serve very quickly, or they will fall.

XXIII.

JELLIES.

In this country culinary skill seems to run to sweet rather than to savory cooking; very few housekeepers but make excellent preserves and cakes, yet the list of sweet dishes manufactured at home is very limited; as soon as anything not in this category is required the caterer is applied to, and he has his list of water-ices, cream-ices, and méringues, with very little variation; sometimes, indeed, a new name appears on the list, but it turns out to be some old friend with a new garnish, or put in a different mould and given an alluring name. There are many delicious sweet dishes not difficult to make when once the processes of making jelly and of freezing are understood (and very many who do not pretend to be good cooks are expert at these two things), and others which do not require even that ability. To put a sweet dish on the table, however, in perfection, especially if it be an iced one, requires the utmost care and skill; the slightest carelessness in packing a frozen pudding, any delay between removing it from the ice and getting it on the dish, will destroy that dull, marble-like appearance it ought to wear when first it makes its entry, although it will gleam with melting sweetness long before it reaches the partakers. Happily there are many delightful sweets which are beautiful in appearance and less depending on atmosphere than any of the family of ices. The simplest of these are fruit jellies.

I spoke just now of the art of making jelly, and many readers may think in using such a term for so simple a thing I am exaggerating, and perhaps "art" is hardly the word, yet there is a daintiness and nicety in making jelly which almost deserves the term.

However, before talking of how sweet dish-

14

es are to be made it is necessary to provide the means by which they are to be redeemed from the commonplace of mere richness and sweetness. The flavorings and liqueurs keep indefinitely if well corked. Orange-flower water, it is true, will lose strength, but when a bottle is first opened, if it is poured off into small vials, and each one corked and *sealed*, it will keep its original strength. The following list of articles kept in store will enable a cook to give her cakes, creams, etc., just that "foreign" flavor that home products so often lack: almonds, almond paste, candied cherries, candied angelica, candied orange, lemon, and citron peels, pistachio-nuts, orange-flower water, rose-water, prepared cochineal, maraschino, ratafia, lemons, extract of vanilla, and sherry.

Several of these things are used principally for decoration; for instance, the candied cherries and angelica and the pistachio-nuts. Consequently, unless the cherries and angelica are required for dessert (to which they are a

showy and delicious addition), a quarter of a
pound at a time is all that need be bought.
Very likely in small cities or country places
these latter articles may not be obtainable.
But they are sold at the large city caterers',
also at the stores which deal in French crys-
tallized fruits—not French *candy* stores—and
can always be sent by mail.

The vanilla should be of the finest quality,
and had better be bought by the ounce or
half-pint from the druggist than from the
grocer. There are good extracts put up, no
doubt, but very many of them are largely
made of tonka-bean, the flavor familiar in
cheap ice-cream, in place of the more expensive vanilla.

In the recipes that will be given the directions will be as minute as possible; but to
prescribe the number of drops required to
flavor a quart of cream would be utterly impossible, the strength of the flavoring used
differing so greatly, even in lemons. Sometimes the juice of half a lemon will be right

for a certain thing, at another the juice of a quarter of one would be too much. This is where judgment must be exercised. If you have a very juicy lemon, although your recipe says the juice of half, you will remember that the average lemon would not yield nearly so much, and that the author had the average lemon in mind. This applies to all flavoring. Sometimes extract of bitter almond is so strong that even a drop would be too much to impart the faint almond flavor which alone is tolerable. In this case the thing to do for fear of spoiling the dish is to pour a half-dozen drops in a teaspoonful of water, and use from that, drop by drop, until the faint flavor desired is attained. In using any flavoring, great care must be taken not to put too much, as anything in the least over-flavored is offensive.

Mould of Apple Jelly.—Peel and cut up a pound of fine-flavored apples (to weigh a pound after preparation); put them in a stewpan with three ounces of granulated sugar, half a pint of water, and the juice and grated rind of a lemon. When cooked to a pulp, pass through a strainer, and stir in one ounce of gelatine that has been dissolved in a gill of water. Color half the apple with *about* half a teaspoonful of cochineal, and fill a border mould with alternate layers of the colored and uncolored apple. When cold, turn out and serve with half a pint of cream whipped solid and piled in the centre.

There is a great difference in the solidity of whipped cream. Sometimes it will be a mere froth that shows a disposition to liquefy, and cannot be piled up. When this is the case there is always a great waste of cream, for at least half will have been left as a milky residue. The reason for this failure of the cream to whip solid is generally because it is too fresh or too warm.

If in proper condition, cream will whip as solid as white of eggs, and leave not a teaspoonful of liquid at the bottom of the bowl; nor will there be the least danger of cream so whipped going back to liquid. It will become sour, but not change its form; and it will take but a few minutes to beat.

Cream intended for whipping should be twenty-four hours old in warm weather, and thirty-six in winter. It should also be thoroughly chilled, and if the day is very warm it would be better to set the bowl containing it on ice while whipping it. Put in the whip, or egg-beater, and *do not* lift the froth off as it rises; it is quite unnecessary if the vessel you use for the cream is large enough. As you see it begin to thicken, which will be after steady beating for five or six minutes, keep on just as you would for white of eggs. When the beater is withdrawn you should be able to cut the cream or pile it any height. If by reason of excessive heat it is slow in reaching the proper consistency, leave the beater in the bowl, and set the whole on the ice until very cold again.

The consistency of jelly should be only just stiff enough to keep form. It should

shake and tremble while being served instead of remaining solid. It requires some
little practice to make sure of this every time,
although exact proportions be given. A tablespoonful difference in the pint or gill measure would, where the gelatine is only just
enough, cause the jelly to "squat"—not an
elegant term, but one that represents the
form of a too soft jelly.

A very exact recipe for plain claret jelly,
and which in proportions serves for any other
unless special mention is made of some variation, is as follows: Three quarters of a pint
of water, one pint of claret, a quarter of a
pint of lemon juice (this makes one quart of
liquid), the rind of one lemon, half an inch
of cinnamon in the stick and two cloves,
one tablespoonful of red currant jelly, two
ounces of gelatine, the whites and shells of
two eggs, a few drops of cochineal, and four
ounces of sugar; put all in a stewpan, the
gelatine having been softened in a little of
the water; whisk over the fire until the whole

boils; then draw it off, let it stand for five to ten minutes; strain through flannel or fine linen *without pressure*, add a few drops of cochineal to brighten the color, and mould for use.

Use great care in selecting cinnamon, for very much that is sold is not the true spice, but a cheaper one (cassia) that resembles it. Cinnamon has a bright tan-color, is rolled many times, and is not much thicker than paper when a piece is unrolled. Cassia is thicker in the roll, a dull brown, and if a piece is broken is like a piece of wood. It is similar in flavor, but much coarser, and has little strength.

XXIV.

JELLIES.—*Continued.*

IF it is kept in mind that two ounces of gelatine to the quart of liquid is the right proportion, and that if even a tablespoonful of flavoring, fruit juice, or what not, is added, exactly the same quantity of other liquid must be omitted, there will not be much danger of formless jelly. Many forget this when not working from an exact recipe, and remembering only that a quart of cream or water or wine requires two ounces of gelatine to set it, they do not deduct for the glass of wine or juice of lemon, etc., they may add for flavoring. Although wine jelly is rather a simple form of sweet, suggestive of innocent country teas, a very little more time than the average housekeeper bestows upon it will convert it into a very elegant

dish.   In the season for fruits there is no
more beautiful ornament for jelly than
these, carefully gathered, with two or three
leaves attached.

Jelly with Fresh Fruits.—Select cherries of
two or three colors if possible, in sprays of
two or three, and on each a leaf or two;
wash them carefully by dipping them in and
out of a bowl of water.   Lay them between
soft cloths to remove all moisture.   Make a
quart of punch jelly in the following way:
Put together a pint of water, a quarter of a
pint of the finest Santa Cruz or Jamaica rum,
a quarter of a pint of sherry, a gill and a half
of lemon juice, the rinds of two lemons, and
the juice of one orange, or, if oranges are not
to be obtained in cherry season, half a gill
more of water, two ounces of gelatine, half
an inch of cinnamon, the whites of two eggs
well beaten and the shells crushed.   Let this
come to a boil over the fire, being well whisk-
ed the while; as soon as it boils draw it to a
cool spot on the range, let it stand five min-

utes, and strain through scalded flannel over a bowl; let it drip, but do not use the least pressure. This jelly must be brilliantly clear. If there is any milky appearance it proves that the jelly did not really boil, and so the eggs had not completely coagulated; in that event boil once more for an instant, and strain again through fresh flannel. Oil a mould that has no design of fruit or vegetable at the bottom, and set it in cracked ice; pour in an inch or two of the jelly when nearly cold. Have the cherries ice cold, and arrange the sprays gracefully with due regard to color, remembering that the best effect must be not upward towards you, but towards the bottom of the mould; thus the underside of the leaves must be upward, etc. Do not put in more fruit than will display itself well. The bunches are to be isolated, not allowed to touch each other, and for this reason it may not be possible to lay more than one cluster at the bottom, if the mould is small there. In this case dispose a bunch

of black cherries and leaves gracefully in the
centre, pour in more jelly, half an inch or so,
then nearer the sides arrange lighter-colored
cherries, two or three clusters, no more. The
fruit is only intended as an ornament. A
jelly that is quite as pretty may be made by
using clusters of red and white, or red, white,
and black currants. The red and white ones
should have two or three young leaves attached, and each cluster be perfect; no black-
currant leaves must be used, as they have a
strong flavor.

Jelly with Candied Fruits.---Make a quart
of maraschino jelly, which is done by omitting the rum, lemon, and cinnamon from the
last recipe, and using in place of rum a gill
of maraschino, and water in place of lemon
juice. The jelly must be very pale. Choose
the fruits of as bright colors as possible—
small green oranges, red cherries, bright yellow mirabelles, angelica perfectly green. Cut
the oranges in half—two or three will suffice
—leave mirabelles and cherries whole; apri-

cots cut in half-moons. The angelica, if cut across a quarter-inch thick, will form rings, but if something more ornamental is desired it can be split lengthwise, softened in hot water, wiped, then tied into small love-knots. Pour into a mould set in ice (the melon shape is excellent for these jellies) an inch of jelly, let it set; then scatter in a few pieces of bright-colored fruit, always the best side downward; pour in an inch more of jelly, and when set more fruit, keeping the brighter pieces towards the side; if you have knots of angelica, put them near the side. Always see that one layer of fruit and jelly is nearly set before adding more.

Although fruits added to jellies in the way just described are chiefly for decorative effect, they do add very greatly to the pleasure of eating them; but jellied fruits, as distinguished from *fruits in jelly*, are a delicious mode of eating fruit, and where it is in abundance afford a pleasant variety.

Jellied Raspberries.—Melt two ounces of

gelatine in a gill of water, squeeze half a pint of currant juice from fresh currants, and crush as many red raspberries as will with the liquid fill a quart measure. It is almost impossible to give definite directions for sugar, as fruits differ so much. Stir in six ounces, then if not sweet enough add more; mould the jelly, and serve with cream.

This is also very nice put in a border mould, the centre filled with whipped cream.

Roman Punch Jellies.—These require stiff paper cases of any of the ornamental kinds used for ice-cream, but they must not flare. Make some maraschino or wine jelly. When it begins to set, pour the jelly into the cases, which must be on ice, so that half the fluid jelly may set before it has time to soak the case. When quite set, very carefully remove the centre, leaving a shell of jelly half an inch thick. The last thing before serving fill the centres with well-frozen Roman-punch ice.

A. Macédoine of fruits, if well managed

and a good assortment of fruits can be had, is a very ornamental way of serving fruit. A mould should have half an inch of maraschino, punch, wine, or lemon jelly poured into it; then some perfect strawberries, or, failing those, red cherries, as many as the jelly will hold together without crowding, no more; then more jelly, and a layer of fruit of another kind (white, if possible), as pineapple cut into stars—a number of small stars can be stamped out of a few thin slices —more jelly, and a ring of dark fruit. Take care that all the finest fruits are used to form the outer rows. When the mould is almost full, with a layer or two of each kind of fruit, fill it up with jelly and set on ice.

Creams are a favorite sweet in Europe, and eaten ice cold are delicious. Too often they are confounded here with blanc-mange, which may mean anything from corn-starch and milk to gelatine and cream, but seldom is improved by the confectioner's art into a really handsome and dainty dish.

Ginger Cream.—Make a custard of a gill of milk, an ounce of powdered sugar, and‧ the beaten yolks of three eggs. Stir in a double boiler until thick. Let it cool. Then add one gill of the syrup from a jar of preserved ginger, and cut up two ounces of the ginger; add three quarters of an ounce of gelatine melted in as little water as possible. Last of all, add half a pint of cream whipped solid. Mix gently and till well blended; pour into a mould, and set on ice.

Neapolitan Cream.— Make a custard of half a pint of milk, the yolks of four eggs, and a tablespoonful and a half of powdered sugar. Let it cool. Cut up three ounces of preserved ginger very small; cook it in a gill of ginger syrup for three minutes. Let it cool also. Decorate the mould with one ounce of dried cherries and leaves, etc., of jelly. Cut the cherries in half, glue them with a little melted jelly to the side and bottom of the mould; cut some jelly in thin slices, or melt it and let it run into thin sheets, which allow to chill, and stamp from them leaves, or whatever shapes you please. Glue these also to the side of the mould in the most effective way your taste can devise. Stir one ounce of gelatine melted in very little water, and half a pint of cream whipped solid, to the custard with which you have already mixed the ginger and syrup. Pour all into the decorated mould, put on ice; and when it is to be turned out wrap a cloth dipped in hot water round the mould; give it a smart slap on both sides, and it will turn out without difficulty.

15

XXV.

Coffee Cream.—Make half a pint of custard with two eggs and half a pint of milk; dissolve an ounce of gelatine and three ounces of sugar in half a gill of strong coffee; add the custard, and strain; whip half a pint of cream quite firm; stir lightly into the custard; when it is cool, pour into a mould, and set on ice. The excellence of this cream depends on the coffee, which must be filtered, not boiled, freshly made, and very strong—three tablespoonfuls of coffee to the half-pint.

Curaçoa Cream.—Make a custard with the yolks of four eggs and half a pint of milk; dissolve half an ounce of gelatine in as little liquid as possible; mix it with two ounces of powdered sugar; add to the custard; then stir in a generous glass of curaçoa, and let the mixture cool, after which add half a pint of cream whipped solid. Stir very lightly together until well blended; then mould and set on ice.

Strawberry Cream.—Hull a pint of quite ripe strawberries; put them on a fine sieve, and sprinkle an ounce of sugar over them; put half an ounce of gelatine into a stewpan with two tablespoonfuls of cold water, two ounces and a half of powdered sugar, and the juice of a lemon, and let it dissolve by gentle heat. Pass the strawberries through the sieve; strain the gelatine, etc., to the strawberry juice, and put to get cold; then add half a pint of cream whipped solid. Stir very lightly to the strawberry juice, etc., when the latter is beginning to set.

Vanilla Cream. — Make a custard with three yolks and one white of egg, and half a pint of milk and three ounces of sugar; melt an ounce of gelatine in two tablespoonfuls of water, strain it to the custard, and mix

well; whip half a pint of cream to a stiff
froth, and stir it gently to the custard and
gelatine; flavor with vanilla. After the vanilla is added, make a couple of spoonfuls of
the custard pink with cochineal or strawberry juice; let this cool in a thin sheet;
stamp from it small clover leaves or lozenges,
not over an inch long and three quarters
broad; decorate the bottom of a mould with
them, using a little gelatine and water to
fasten them; set the mould in chopped ice,
and about half-way up put four or five of
the pink pieces; take great care there is no
inequality as to height or distance (slovenly
decoration is worse than none). When the
lozenges are quite secure in their places, pour
in the cream. It is needless to repeat this
form of decoration of creams, they can be
varied so infinitely by individual taste, but
as a rule they should be decorated only with
small forms cut out of bright-colored jelly,
or of cream colored pink, orange, pistache
green, or brown. Candied fruits are not ef-

fective, although sometimes used, unless the cream itself has fruit in it.

Pistache Cream.—Half an ounce of gelatine, two ounces of powdered sugar; melt the gelatine in a gill of water, then add the sugar, a glass of sherry, and a glass of kirsch. Whip half a pint of thick cream solid, and when the gelatine is cold and beginning to thicken stir the cream to it very lightly, and at the same time two ounces of pistachio-nuts, blanched and chopped fine, with enough vegetable green coloring to make the cream a shade or two lighter in color than the nuts. This cream must be stirred lightly on ice after the nuts are added, till thick enough for them not to sink.

Almond Cream.—Half an ounce of gelatine melted in a gill of water with two ounces of sugar and a glass of sherry; grate four ounces of almond paste into it, and stir in a double boiler or bowl set in boiling water until dissolved, or at least until there are no lumps. Let this get cool. Whip a pint and a gill of cream solid, and stir to the mixture. Decorate a mould with any red jelly, pour the mixture in, and set on ice. In consequence of the variation in the strength of gelatine, in making any of these creams try a little on ice in a saucer before pouring into a mould, then add more cream or gelatine as required.

Cold Puddings and Frozen Puddings.—Some of these "puddings" might just as appropriately be called creams; however, fashion ordains that they shall be puddings. One of the newest is the

Jubilee Pudding.—Make a pint of claret jelly; pour it into a small border mould; whip half a pint of cream in which is a quarter of an ounce of dissolved gelatine. When it is whipped solid, stir in one ounce of preserved or candied cherries, one ounce of candied angelica, one ounce of preserved ginger, and one ounce of preserved apricot—the ginger and angelica cut small. Set on ice; then turn out. Pile the whipped cream and fruit in the centre, and decorate according to fancy.

Cold Soufflé Pudding à la Princesse.—
Melt half an ounce of gelatine in a gill of
cream; set in boiling water till dissolved;
beat the yolks of three eggs well, and add to
the milk; when well mixed, put the custard
into a double boiler till it thickens—it must
not boil. Pour it into a bowl, and add a gill
of apricot preserve, made into a purée by
rubbing through a sieve with half a gill of
orange juice, two ounces of sugar, a little
lemon juice, and cochineal to color it a very
delicate pink. Beat the whites of four eggs
till they will not slip; stir them in very lightly with an upward motion of the spoon, the
object being to keep the white of egg from
falling, yet the whole must be thoroughly
mixed. Stir till nearly cold before putting
the soufflé in a mould to set.

Imperial Rice Pudding.—Pour a quarter
of a pint of clear white jelly into a quart
mould, turning the mould about so that the
jelly covers every part; this jelly serves to
keep the ornaments in place. Cover the in-

side of the mould with an ounce of candied cherries split and half an ounce of angelica cut into thin rings. Stew a quarter of a pound of rice in a pint of milk till tender; when cool, add half a pint of whipped cream, a quarter of an ounce of gelatine melted in a little water, a quarter of a pound of powdered sugar, and a teaspoonful of vanilla. When it is all well mixed, turn the preparation into the mould, and set on ice. When firm, turn out of the mould, and serve with a purée of apricots.

Diplomatic Pudding.—Make a quart of custard in the following way: Put the yolks of four eggs and the white of one into a bowl, and mix well with a wooden spoon; stir in half a pint of milk, and strain all into a double boiler or a pitcher; add two ounces of sugar, and stand the pitcher (unless you have the double boiler) in a saucepan of boiling water, and stir the custard over the fire until it thickens, but it must not boil; remove from the fire; stir in a tablespoonful of brandy and a little vanilla. Line a plain mould with half a pint of wine jelly; this is done by pouring a little in at a time when it is half fluid, rolling the mould about on ice, and as soon as one coat adheres, pour in more, until the mould is evenly coated; decorate it with half an ounce of candied cherries and half an ounce of angelica—the cherries split and the angelica cut. Melt an ounce of gelatine and two ounces of sugar in a gill of water; stir it into the custard with a gill of thick cream; stir till cool; then add an ounce more cherries, half an ounce of angelica, and half an ounce of citron, all chopped small. Pour this gently into the mould you have decorated, set on ice, turn out and serve.

Cold Cabinet Pudding.— Ornament the bottom of a pint mould with candied cherries and angelica; split half a dozen lady-fingers; line the sides of the mould very evenly with them, arranging them alternately back and front against the mould; put in two ounces of ratafias (these are tiny macaroons about the size of a five-cent piece, of high flavor, and to be obtained at the pastry-cooks' who make foreign specialties; some grocers also import them); put four yolks of eggs into a bowl; stir them; then add half a pint of milk; pour this custard into a double boiler, and stir until it thickens, taking care that it does not curdle. Melt half an ounce of gelatine in a very little water; strain it to the custard. When the latter cools, add half a gill of thick, fresh cream, two ounces of sugar, and a teaspoonful of vanilla; mix all well, and pour carefully into the mould without disturbing the lining of cake. Put the mould on ice, and, when set, turn out and serve.

XXVI.

Nut creams, with the exception of almond, are not very well known, but are so delicious that they ought to be. One reason perhaps is that it is not generally known that kernels of nuts, such as hazel-nuts, walnuts, hickory-nuts, etc., can be bought by the pound at confectioners' supply stores. This, of course, saves the tedious work of cracking and shelling. To use with creams or for frozen puddings the nuts must be pounded very well, with very little white of egg—just enough to moisten and render the process easy.

Cocoanut Cream. — Grate a fresh, sweet cocoanut (having first peeled, washed, and wiped it *dry*); mix with it an ounce of sugar; melt in as little water as possible three quarters of an ounce of gelatine; whip the whites of three eggs, mix them with half a pint of milk, and stir over the fire until the custard thickens; sweeten with four table-spoonfuls of sugar. Stir the gelatine and a full half-pint of grated cocoanut with the cocoanut milk into the custard. Whip half a pint of thick cream solid, and stir it very carefully into the custard; when the latter is quite cold, but before it sets, flavor with a little vanilla or lemon extract. Mould and set on ice.

Hazel-nut Cream.—Put a pint of hazel-nut kernels into a cool oven until they are thoroughly dry and rather hot (they must not become too hot, or they will change flavor); then rub them between two coarse cloths to get rid of as much as possible of the skin (it cannot be entirely removed); blow away the loose hulls, and pound the nuts to a paste with a little white of egg. Make a custard with the yolks of three eggs and half a pint of milk; dissolve half an ounce of gelatine in a gill of water, mix with six ounces of powdered sugar, and add to the custard when nearly cool. Stir in the hazel-nut paste, taking care that it is well mixed with the custard, and add a half-pint of cream whipped solid; flavor with vanilla, or you may omit flavoring, the hazel-nut being sufficient for many people. Mould and set on ice.

This cream and the two that follow are flecked with brown, for which reason it may be colored brown with caramel, although I prefer it uncolored, the specks being no more objectionable than the vanilla seeds one rejoices to see in ice-cream.

Walnut or Hickory-nut Cream. — Pound one pint of either of these nuts, after rubbing them well in a cloth, make the same custard as for hazel-nut cream, stir in the walnut or hickory-nut paste till smooth, add the whipped cream, color a pale pink with cochineal, and flavor faintly with rum or vanilla. Mould, set on ice, and serve with whipped cream flavored slightly with rum.

Bohemian Jelly Creams.—These may be

made of any flavor, according to the jelly
you use. It may be jelly of fruit or liqueur.
If fresh fruit is used for jelly, the juice must
be expressed, and well-sweetened gelatine
added in the proportion of an ounce to the
pint. If jam or marmalade is used, a pint
of water is added and the same amount of
gelatine, with the juice of half a lemon to the
pint. Water, jam, and dissolved gelatine
must be mixed quickly and passed through
a sieve; either must be stirred in a bowl set
in ice till quite cold and beginning to thick-
en; then stir in gently and quickly three-
quarters of a pint of cream whipped solid;
pour the mixture into the mould, which must
be set in ice. Cover well, and keep on ice
till needed.

Frangipanni Iced Pudding.—Grate six
ounces of almond paste to crumbs; then on
a smaller grater grate four or six bitter almonds blanched and dried; pound a dozen
candied orange-flower petals with three-
quarters of a pound of powdered sugar; put

all into a stewpan with the yolks of eight eggs, and beat them very well together. In another stewpan have a pint and a half of boiling milk, which must be poured over the other ingredients by degrees, keeping them well stirred. Place it over the fire, stirring until it thickens and adheres to the back of the spoon; rub this all through a coarse sieve, add a glass of sherry, and when cold pour the mixture into the freezer; when half frozen add a pint and a half of whipped cream, and when quite frozen fill a pudding mould, bury it in ice and salt, and serve as you would Nesselrode pudding.

Iced Cabinet Pudding.—Cut a stale sponge cake into slices half an inch thick and rather smaller than the mould you intend to use for the pudding; lay the slices of cake to soak in brandy flavored with noyau; decorate the bottom and sides of the mould with candied fruits, split cherries, angelica rings, the same of green oranges, and little diamonds of ginger, with a few whole ratafias, dipping them in jelly to make them adhere; lay in one slice of cake, then cherries and ratafias, another slice of cake, and so on, until the mould is three parts full. Make a quart of custard with six yolks of eggs, three tablespoonfuls of sugar, and an ounce of gelatine; when this is cold pour part into the mould, which must close hermetically; pack it in salt and ice for at least two hours; when you wish to turn it out, dip it a minute in lukewarm water. Keep the remaining custard on ice, flavor it with sherry or rum, beat it up, pour it around the pudding, and strew it with chopped pistachio-nuts.

Ice Pudding.—Make a custard with a pint and a half of milk, one whole egg and the yolks of four others, and a quarter of a pound of sugar; when cold, add half a glass of brandy, a glass of maraschino, an ounce of citron cut fine, a quarter of a pound of dried fruits, and an ounce of pistachio-nuts, the fruits cut up in small pieces, the pistachio-nuts blanched and split; mix well; and lastly add half a pint of whipped cream. When well frozen, pack into a pudding mould, and bury in ice and salt till wanted.

Bombay Ice Pudding.—Line a plain mould with Roman-punch ice an inch thick, keeping it bedded nearly to the brim in ice and salt while you do it; then fill the centre with the following mixture: a pint of cocoanut grated very fine, mixed with a pint of ice-cream; take great care that the cocoanut is ice-cold before you mix it in, or it will melt the ice-cream. When the mould is filled within an inch of the top, cover it with Roman punch, close the mould hermetically, and bury in ice. These puddings, where two kinds of ice are used, must only be attempted after one has learned to pack plain ice-cream with success.

Iced Jelly Pudding.—Make a custard with a pint of boiling cream, three ounces of sugar, and the yolks of four eggs beaten; pour the cream to the eggs very carefully, stirring it in by degrees. Have ready a quarter of an

16

ounce of gelatine dissolved in very little milk, mix it in, and put the vessel containing the custard in a stewpan of boiling water, and stir till it just thickens; then whisk it until nearly cold. Mask a quart mould with jelly an inch thick—any favorite *red* jelly, or a pale one tinted. Directions have already been given how the inside of a mould is to be coated with jelly. There is an easier but extravagant way, namely, to fill the mould with jelly, then scoop out the centre neatly, leaving a shell of jelly an inch thick. The centre, of course, might be made hot and bottled for another occasion, or to make Bohemian cream jellies. When the mould is masked, fill it with the custard, which must be half frozen; then cover securely, and pack in ice and salt at least five hours before it is served.

XXVII

Filbert and Wine Iced Pudding.—To one pint of cream put four tablespoonfuls of sugar and two glasses of fine sherry. The cream must be perfectly sweet, but should be at least twenty-four hours old, and be ice cold. Whip this solid; then freeze. Put a pint of filberts in a cool oven till the skins will nearly all rub off; put them between two coarse cloths, and rub as much as possible of the brown coating off them; pound them to a paste with a little thick cream, mix four ounces of sugar with the nuts, and then blend the whole with enough thick custard to make a very thick batter; flavor with lemon or vanilla, or not, as you choose; freeze. Line a plain mould with the frozen wine cream an inch thick; then fill in the centre with the frozen filberts well pressed in; cover tight, and pack in ice and salt for three hours, or until wanted. This pudding can be made of walnuts and port-wine cream.

Iced Custard with Fruit.—Flavor one pint of cream with any liqueur you prefer; beat twelve eggs thoroughly; strain them; boil the cream with five ounces of sugar, and when it is just off the boil pour it, little by little, to the eggs; add a quarter of an ounce of gelatine that has been dissolved in very little water and strained to the custard; whisk until cold; have ready a mould masked with candied fruits. To mask, set the mould in a pan of cracked ice, and dip each piece of fruit in strong melted jelly; build up from the bottom of the mould having all the fruits, cut about the thickness of a split candied cherry and near the size, arranged with a view to a good effect when the mould shall be turned out. Half freeze the custard, and pour it in the mould three inches high; throw in some of the trimmings

of candied fruit chopped fine. When set,
add more custard, then more fruit, until the
mould is full. Let it stand in ice at least
five hours before it is wanted.

Rice à la Princesse.—Let some rice swell
in water until quite tender; proportion, one
cup of rice to two (scant) of water; then butter a saucepan; put the rice into it, with half
a pint of milk; let it stew gently till it will
mash; the milk must have all been absorbed;
sweeten with three tablespoonfuls of sugar.
Mix with this a gill of apricot jam, a teaspoonful of vanilla, and half a pint of whipped
cream; freeze; when well frozen, pack in a
mould and bury in ice and salt. Pound a
dozen macaroons; stir them into a pint of
whipped cream; let the mixture be put on
ice. When the pudding is turned out of the
mould, cover with the macaroon cream, and
decorate the dish with cubes of peach or
apricot jelly.

Chocolate Cream Pudding.—Boil a quarter
of a pound of the finest vanilla chocolate in

half a pint of milk, whisking it well till it boils; dissolve in it two tablespoonfuls of powdered sugar. Beat three half-pints of cream and three tablespoonfuls of sugar solid while the chocolate cools; when it is *ice* cold mix in one half the beaten cream, and freeze. Line a plain mould with the frozen chocolate (the remainder of the whipped cream should have been kept in cracked ice and salt, so as to be ice cold); fill up the centre of the mould with the cream, cover tight, and bury in salt and ice.

Ice-Creams and Ices.—There are so many ways of making ice-cream that all one can do is to indicate the one or two best, and certainly the *very* best is the simplest, and there is no dessert so easy to prepare in hot weather as this, since there is no work over the fire. The only trouble is breaking the ice and turning the machine for some twenty minutes, which can be done by a child.

Simplest Fruit Ice-Cream.—Mash two pounds of strawberries or raspberries, put to them half a pound of powdered sugar, and let them remain in a cold place two or three hours, so that the juice may run; then strain the juice to a quart of thick sweet cream and another half pound of sugar, with the juice of half a lemon; stir, and pour cream and fruit juice into the freezer, which must be packed with ice and rock-salt in about equal quantities, the ice being broken quite small. Let the cream remain standing in the freezer a few minutes before you begin to turn; then freeze, letting off the water, and filling anew with ice and salt if necessary. Stir the cream down as it forms, and keep on turning five or ten minutes after it is actually necessary. This extra working insures that extreme smoothness characteristic of Italian and French ice-cream. If you are not expert in freezing, be satisfied not to pack your cream in a mould for the first few times. Take out the paddle of the freezer, press the ice compactly down in the freezer, cover, and see that the ice and salt are sufficient and free from water. In two hours you can turn the ice out of the freezer in a round column or loaf that will be quite as sightly as the oblong square one frequently gets from the caterer. Many people think that simply freezing the pure cream produces the loose, frothy cream found at inferior confectioners', but this is not the case; pure cream frozen results in a firm smooth mass which cuts like butter.

I have given the formula for raspberry and strawberry cream only, but any fruit juice may be substituted, varying the quantity of sugar as required.

When it is desirable to freeze the fruit in the cream instead of the juice, it must not be added until the cream is frozen. Stir in raspberries, strawberries, chopped pineapple, banana, or peaches just before the ice is ready to pack down; otherwise the fruit, being full of water, will freeze into hard knots.

Tutti-frutti Ice-Cream being made from chopped candied fruit, this precaution is not necessary; the fruit may be added at any time during the freezing, or stirred in last, as you please.

I have given the simplest and best method of making ice-cream, yet the way most in use is to add custard; and French cooks always use "méringue paste," claiming that it insures a smoothness and lightness nothing else can give.

Custard for Ice-Cream.—This is made as any other custard, except that double the amount of sugar is allowed for everything that is to be frozen. It may be made of from three to six eggs to a pint of milk, as you prefer. This must be ice cold before you put it in the freezer.

Ice-Cream with Eggs.—One pint of milk, three eggs, leaving out one white, half a pound of sugar (if acid fruit is to be added, it may require more for some tastes). Make a custard of these materials, and half freeze it; then add a pint of cream whipped solid. Stir in well and finish freezing, turning the handle some few minutes after it gets pretty stiff, if there is a strong enough hand near to do it.

In making varieties of ice-cream you have only to consider the fitness of the articles you use; for instance, any sort of fruit may be added, with the exception of lemons. Fleshy fruits, such as pineapple, peaches, pears, etc., are usually mixed with the cream uncooked in this country; abroad this is only done with soft fruits, such as raspberries, blackberries, oranges, and such as will mash through a colander. Others are very slight-ly stewed in rich syrup (as nearly their own juice as possible), then pulped and mixed through when the cream is nearly frozen.

In winter, fruit jams, and especially jellies, are very pleasant in ice-cream; they always require a little lemon juice to restore some of the natural sharpness of fresh fruit. A tumbler of red currant jelly turned into a pint of ice-cream is delicious, and gives a pretty, faint

pink tint. The method is just the same whether for custard and cream or cream alone.

The méringue paste alluded to as used by
foreign confectioners is made by beating the
white of an egg with a tablespoonful of powdered sugar until stiff.

Grilled Almond Ice-Cream.—Make a quart
of ice-cream; grill some almonds in the following way : Blanch four ounces of almonds,
dry them in a hot spot till they are brittle;
then put in a thick saucepan or sauté pan
four ounces of sugar and a gill of water; let
them boil five minutes; throw in the almonds; stir them till part of the sugar adheres and they begin to turn yellow. Take
them up, chop them, and when quite cold stir
them into the ice-cream, which should be
flavored with vanilla.

XXVIII.

To those very fond of tea, ice-cream made with it is very acceptable, and is very much used at English garden parties.

Tea Ice-Cream.—To one pound of granulated sugar put a pint of strong green tea, a pint and a half of cream, and two quarts of rich milk, and a very little cinnamon water. Let the whole simmer one minute, not stirring, but keeping the mixture in motion by gently swinging the saucepan. Freeze as usual. This recipe may be used for coffee and chocolate; it will make a large quantity, and for a medium-sized family one quarter will suffice.

Chinese Ice.—Beat the yolks of fifteen eggs with three quarters of a pound of powdered sugar; pound four ounces of pistachio-nuts

(blanched) with the white of an egg; put to
it three gills of water; stir it over the fire in
a double boiler till it is as thick as cream;
take great care that it does not boil. Color
it green, or part green and part yellow; flavor as you please; cut up a couple of candied
Chinese oranges small and a little preserved
ginger, and freeze.

Water-Ices.—These are exceedingly simple, and no more elegant form of refreshment
can be offered than a plate of well-frozen or
a tumbler of half-frozen water-ice. It is acceptable when ice-cream would be too heavy,
and can be offered at the simplest country
afternoon tea, or during a call, without the
seeming ostentation of ice-cream.

Ginger Water-Ice (to serve as a beverage
if preferred).—Take six ounces of preserved
ginger, free from fibre; pound it; make two
quarts of lemonade by paring eight or ten
lemons so thinly that the knife-blade shows
through the yellow; put the peel of three
in a pitcher with a pound and a quarter of

sugar; pour two quarts of boiling water on them, and cover; squeeze and strain the juice from the lemons, add to the water, and when cold stir in the pounded ginger, with the méringue paste made with the whites of four eggs. Freeze it. If for drinking, only half freeze, work only enough to make it like half-melting snow, and use only sugar enough to make a refreshing drink. Italians call this *granito*, and it is a form of ice not often met with in this country.

Pineapple Water-Ice.—This can be readily made of canned pineapple when the fresh fruit is out of season. Peel a pineapple; grate it into a mortar; then pound it well with six ounces of sugar; let it stand covered for an hour; add the juice of five oranges, and a pint and a half of syrup boiled to the little thread, or *à lissé*. (This syrup is much used in making water-ices, punches, etc. It is sugar and water boiled till it forms a little thread between thumb and finger.) Mix well and freeze. If canned fruit is used, you need less sugar, and substitute lemon for half the orange juice.

Almond Water-Ice.—Take one pound of almond paste, a pint and a half of water, and three quarters of a pound of sugar; grate the paste; then stir till quite dissolved. Flavor with vanilla or raspberry; stir in the whites of two eggs and some candied fruits cut up small. Freeze as usual.

Cinnamon Water-Ice.—This is a German ice, and very much liked by those who are fond of the flavor. Pound an ounce of the finest quality of cinnamon in the stick, put it into a pint and a half of boiling water, and cover it well; when it is cold add a quart of syrup (the little thread) and the well-beaten whites of two eggs, and freeze it.

Pistachio Water-Ice.—Blanch and pound a pound of pistachio-nuts, using the white of an egg to moisten; mix with a quart of syrup *à lissé.* Heighten the color, if too pale, with spinach coloring, and flavor to taste. (Pistachio-nuts have no flavor of their own, astonishing as the fact may seem to those who have heard frequently of pistachio flavor.) Freeze as usual.

Apricot Water-Ice.—There is no more delicious water-ice than this if fine-flavored apricots are used. The canned ones are excellent for the purpose. Pulp two pounds of apricots through a sieve or jelly press; grate or pound very fine five or six bitter almonds; mix with the pulp the juice of the apricots (from the can), and a pint and a half of syrup, and the beaten whites of three eggs made into a paste with three tablespoonfuls of powdered sugar; stir all well, and freeze. This ice ought to be the color of apricots; if too pale, add a very little saffron coloring.

Currant Water-Ice. — A pint of currant juice, a pint of syrup, and the whites of three eggs made into méringue paste. Freeze as usual. Any of these water-ices can be half frozen as *graniti*, and served in glasses as *granito*, the only exceptions being the almond and pistachio water-ices.

Graniti are also made of various kinds of light punches by adding to a quart of the usual punch recipe a quart of sweetened water. Any summer beverage made from fruit juice can be turned into a *granito*, by half freezing, in either of the following ways :

To Freeze Graniti.—Mix the beverage you intend to freeze, for instance, we will say, a pint of very strong, clear, bright coffee and half a pint of syrup *à lissé*. Put them into the freezer and turn ; as it becomes frozen up the sides, scrape it down with a spoon, and remember, as soon as it resembles snowy water (not white, of course) it is frozen enough. It must be just liquid enough to pour out.

There is a second way of freezing *graniti* by which they can be put on the table in the vessel in which they were frozen. Place the mixture in wide-mouthed water-bottles, twirl them round in ice and salt, and, as the contents become frozen on the inside of the bot-

17

tle, scrape down with a narrow wooden stick or spatula. When frozen in perfection the bottle should seem half filled with tiny crystals.

Claret Granito.—To one pint of orangeade add a bottle of claret. Half freeze.

Sherry Granito.—To one quart of lemonade add a bottle of sherry, and freeze.

The housekeeper who lives far from a large city will need materials for many of the recipes given in these papers and others which she will meet with in books on high-class cooking. Many of these can be sent for by mail, and all, of course, by express; but it will often not seem worth while to send perhaps for one small bottle that we may lack. For this reason I give a few directions for preparing very tolerable imitations of liqueurs, which, however, unless it were a question of economy, it might not be worth while doing if within reach of stores.

Curaçoa.—Pare a dozen and a half of deadripe oranges so thin that you can see the knife pass under the rind; pound one dram of finest cinnamon and half a dram of mace; put them to steep for fifteen days in a gallon of pure alcohol, shaking it every day. Make a clarified syrup of four pounds of sugar and one quart of water well boiled and skimmed; add this to the curaçoa. Rub up in a mortar one dram of potash with a teaspoonful of the liqueur; when well mixed add it, and then do the same with a dram of alum. Shake well, and in an hour or two filter through thin muslin. It will be ready for use in a week.

Maraschino.—Bruise two ounces of cherry kernels and one of bitter almonds; put them in a deep jar with the thin outer rind of twelve oranges and five lemons. Steep in one gallon of English gin or alcohol. Let the whole stand a fortnight, then filter and bottle.

Ratafia.—Blanch the kernels of uncooked peaches or apricots, and when you have two ounces pound them, and pour to them a quart of gin or alcohol and the thin yellow rind of two lemons. Sweeten with a pound of white sugar-candy, and leave the whole for two months; then filter and bottle for use.

Candied Orange and Lemon Peels.—These are invaluable both as decoration for certain desserts and for culinary purposes, and as they are not always to be found except in the larger cities, the method of preparing them is here given: Throw the peels into salt and water, all pulp being removed, but the white part must be left untouched; in fact, the thicker the peel the better for the purpose, thin-skinned oranges being of no use for candying. Let them remain in the salt and water from nine days to three weeks; then wash them, put them on the fire in cold water, and let them boil till perfectly tender, yet they must not be mushy. During the time they are boiling change the water until it no longer tastes salt. Lemon-peels may take from three to four hours' boiling, orange-peels less; but remember, should the lemon-peel not be quite tender, it will harden when it goes into syrup, and instead of a rich sweetmeat there will be only woody chips. Drain the peels, and make a thin syrup of a pint of water to each pound of sugar. Let it boil five minutes; then throw in the peels; they must boil gently in this until they are clear and the syrup has become thick — almost boiled away, in fact. Now make another syrup, half a pint of water to two pounds of sugar; let it boil till clear and till there is a short hair from the fork. Now put in the peels (which must have been drained from the other syrup); remove from the fire; stir them round till the syrup looks whitish; then lift each piece out and lay it on a dish on which granulated sugar has been freely sprinkled.

Both orange and lemon peels are candied by the same process, but they must never be put in the same vessel of salt and water, nor must they be candied together, or the distinctive flavors would be lost.

XXIX.

UNDER this head I intend to give a few sweets that seem to me unusually good, although they may not always be novel, except in manner of serving. A compote of fruit has nothing new about it, yet by the way in which it is served it may simply be " stewed fruit," or it may be a dish fit to find a place even in choice cookery.

In making compotes great care must be taken to preserve the shape and color of the fruits. In order to do this they must be quickly peeled and dipped into strong lemon juice and water, and dropped into syrup in which also a little lemon juice has been squeezed. Pass the blade of the knife over its own marks to obliterate the appearance of peeling. Peaches and apricots may be boiled up without peeling, and (unless they are allowed to get too soft) the skins will be removed easily. It will be observed that hard fruits such as apples are simmered in thin syrup to get tender, while rich soft fruits are dropped into syrup boiled to candy height.

Apple Compote No. 1.— Cut up and boil half a dozen apples in a pint of water. When they are quite soft strain the juice from them without squeezing; put to it half a pound of granulated sugar and the zest of a lemon (the zest is the peel so thin that the knife blade can be seen through it while paring), together with the juice. Let this syrup boil for a minute; skim it. Then pare half a dozen fine cooking apples; core them; let them boil gently in the syrup until quite tender, but not in danger of breaking. Take them up on a perforated skimmer. When cold, put the apples into a compote dish. Boil the juice to a jelly; pour part of it over the apples; dip a plate in cold water, drain

it, and then pour out the rest of the jelly into
it: it should only cover it about the thickness of thick paper. When stiff, warm the
under-side of the plate *very slightly*, pass a
broad thin knife under, and lay the sheet of
jelly over the apples in the compote dish.

Apple Compote No. 2.—Prepare the apples
as in last recipe, but before the last sheet of
jelly is laid over them ornament with rings
and leaves of angelica, and any red jelly or
preserve cut in thin slices and stamped out
with tiny tin cutters in leaves, stars, or fancy
shapes (stiff red currant jelly or red quince
may be used); decorate thus each apple;
then lay the thin sheet of apple jelly over all.

Compote of Stuffed Apples.—Prepare the
apples as in the foregoing recipes, taking
care to core them all through without splitting the apple. When the apples are done,
fill the centre with orange marmalade or
apricot preserve. Boil the syrup down till
it will glaze; pour it over the apples when
they are ice-cold, the syrup also only warm

enough to remain liquid. By this means
the rich coating will remain over the apples,
while if both were warm it would run off.

Compote of Apples or Pears Grillé.—If you
have any apples or pears left from a compote
(or you may, of course, prepare them especially), put them into a frying or sauté pan over
a brisk fire; put with them any syrup there
may be and a cup of sugar just dissolved in
water; boil rapidly down to a pale caramel,
rolling the apples with a fork so that they
become covered with the caramel. Take
great care that the syrup does not burn; remove it from the fire the moment it begins
to change color. The apples should now have
an even glossy surface; as each is finished
put it at once into the compotier. Pour a little curaçoa syrup round just before sending
to table.

Compote of Apple Marmalade. — This is
not so troublesome to make as it sounds, especially to any one who has made glacé nuts
—a very general accomplishment nowadays.

Reduce some apple marmalade by leaving it for an hour or two in a double boiler; the water boiling round it will evaporate moisture without danger of burning. Stir occasionally, and when the marmalade is so reduced that it will make a firm paste when cold (try a little in a saucer on ice), color one half pink with cochineal. Spread half an inch thick on plates slightly oiled ; when stiff and cold, cut out the marmalade into squares, ovals, diamonds, leaves, etc., with tin cutters. Boil a pound of sugar with a gill of water to the crack—that is, until a teaspoonful dropped in ice-water will crack between the teeth. Oil a fork and a large dish, and use the fork to drop the pieces of marmalade into the candy ; lift them out quickly, and lay them on the dish, which will be better if it is set on ice. When they are cold, dish them in a pyramid, the pink to contrast with the white effectively. Pour a little liqueur-flavored syrup round the base of the fruit.

Compote of Pears (white).—Use any fine-flavored dessert pears. Cut them in halves, core, pare, and trim neatly, and simmer them in syrup (a pound of sugar and juice of half a lemon to a pint of water) till they are tender, yet firm to the touch. Dish the pieces, keeping them close to each other. Lay a thin sheet of apple jelly over them, and the syrup, boiled down till rich and thick, round them.

A Pink Compote is prepared in the same way, the only difference being that a very few drops of cochineal are added to the syrup before the pears go in. Decorate with angelica.

Pears à la Princesse. Select seven pears of the best quality, without blemish, and of equal size; pare them with great care; stand them close together in a saucepan, with weak acidulated syrup to cover them; simmer slowly till quite tender, but yet firm to the touch; take them up, leaving the syrup to boil down. When cold, cut the stalk end off each pear about an inch deep, or so as to leave about an inch of surface, on which place a ring of angelica (simply cut angelica crosswise and it forms rings, being tubular); if the rings are flattened, lay them in syrup; when softened bend them round and lay one on each pear; then, if in season, dip a fine strawberry or stoned red cherry in the hot syrup and lay it on the ring of angelica. Cut strips of angelica and run them through the strawberry down to the pear, both to hold the decoration in place and to represent the stalk; dish them standing; when dished up, pour some syrup, boiled till thick and rich, over the seven pears. When fresh fruit is not in season for decoration, use candied cherries.

Variegated Compote of Pears.—This is a pretty dish. Prepare some pears as in the last recipe, except that the tops are not to be cut off; color half the number a pale pink by adding a few drops of cochineal to the syrup in which they are simmered; dress them alternately, a pink pear and a white one, in the compotier; pour over each the pink and white syrup in which they were cooked, and pour syrup flavored with vanilla round them.

Compote of Oranges.—Divide six oranges in halves; first cut out the centre string of pith, pick all pips out carefully, and with a very sharp knife pare off the peel of the orange down to the naked transparent pulp; in this way you get rid of the whole of the white outside skin. Place the halves as you do them in a bowl; pour over them some hot syrup boiled *à lissé*, flavored with orange peel, rubbed with lump sugar, and previously dissolved in the syrup; a very little lemon juice should be added if the oranges are very sweet. Let them steep a few minutes; then remove them; then build the oranges into a pyramid on the compotier, and the last thing before going to table pour the syrup, well boiled and cold, over them.

Chestnut Compote.—Take the largest French or Spanish chestnuts, make slits in the peel, and boil till tender; take off the shell, and press them flat without breaking;

lay them in a saucepan; pour over them thick syrup; put them in the oven, but do not let them boil; when they look quite clear take them up, put them into the compotier, boil the syrup to candy height, squeeze into the compotier the juice of an orange, and pour the candy over the chestnuts.

Chestnut Compote No. 2.—Prepare the nuts as in last recipe; put the yolks of three eggs in a saucepan; stir gradually to them a pint of cream; cook a quarter of a pound of sugar to the crack, with a few dried orange flowers; the minute the candy begins to get yellowish pour it into the cream, stirring constantly, and let it come to boiling-point; then strain the cream over the chestnuts.

XXX.

STRAWBERRIES, raspberries, currants, etc., need very little cooking, and that little in high candy. If it is understood that strong syrup tends to make fruit firm, and weak syrup to make it tender, it will be seen why all soft fruit, in order to keep its shape, should be dropped into candy boiled till brittle, and why apples and other hard fruits should be first stewed in weak syrup until soft; yet there are degrees; for instance, hard peaches require thin syrup, and very luscious ones must be put into syrup that is very near candy. This is also the case with pears. Be guided as to the strength of the syrup by the kind of fruit. Avoid fruit that is very ripe, because the syrup from it will not jelly readily.

Compote of Strawberries.—Select a quart of fine large berries, rather under than over ripe; boil three quarters of a pound of sugar to the crack; drop the strawberries into the syrup after it is removed from the fire; return them to the range; let them boil gently once; take out the berries most carefully with the skimmer; lay them on the compotier; boil the syrup fast, skimming it carefully; then pour it over the fruit.

Compote of Cherries is made in the same way, with the finest red cherries, only they require to boil up several times. When clear, drain them with the skimmer; lay them in the compote dishes; add a gill of red currant juice to the syrup; boil it till it is a weak jelly; then throw it over the cherries when nearly cold.

Orange Baskets Filled with Fruits.—Select seven oranges, not too large, but all the same size. With a very sharp knife pare the fruit as thin as possible—so thin that it still remains yellow, and only the shining outer surface is removed (in fact, it may be lightly grated off, but that is more trouble), to render them transparent; cut two quarters out of the upper part of the orange, so as to leave a narrow band half an inch wide, which will form the handle; pass the knife carefully round inside the band, so as to remove the strip of pulp. With the bowl of a teaspoon detach the remaining pulp from the inside without in any way damaging the shape of the basket. As you prepare them, drop them in a saucepan of cold water, and then put them into boiling water, and simmer three minutes gently. This is only to soften the peel and enable you to stamp out the edges with a perforating cutter, if you have one, which will give them an open-work effect; if not, just scallop them with scissors, and snip out a sort of trellis-work to increase the basket effect. Put them into a preserving-kettle with weak syrup *à lissé*, boil them gently till they look clear, then put them aside in the syrup till next day;

18

boil the syrup twice alone at intervals of several hours, and throw it over the baskets. These baskets may be kept ready prepared for months by putting them in wide jars and covering them with syrup. When required for use, they must be taken out, drained thoroughly, and then filled with a variety of small fruits, such as cherries, strawberries, currants, etc., which have been mixed with a little apple or orange jelly. In winter, ambrosia—a mixture of cut-up banana, grated cocoa-nut, orange quarters, etc.—may be served in them, or a mixture of preserved fruits that are firm, such as Chinese oranges, limes, ginger, etc. In all cases serve them on a compote dish, and throw over them syrup flavored with maraschino.

Lemon Baskets are prepared precisely as the orange baskets, but they require longer boiling, and the syrup they are served with should be flavored with citronelle or the rasped peel of green limes.

Orange Baskets Glacé. — These are not

much more trouble than the baskets simply preserved, but if successfully done they can be very effectively filled with candies or ice-cream. Prepare the baskets as in last recipe, drain them on a napkin, very carefully remove all moisture from the inside, and set them over a register, or in an oven with the door open, to dry. Boil two pounds of sugar with a pint of water and two tablespoonfuls of vinegar till it begins to change color (this is some little time after the brittle stage is reached, and is called caramel); lightly oil the skimmer, and drop a basket in the candy; remove as quickly as possible, but see that the whole is well coated, yet has as little superfluous candy as possible, for which reason the baskets must be warm when they are dipped, also the skimmer. You must not leave the candy on the fire after it *begins* to change color, but the work of coating the baskets had better be done quite near the fire, with the pot containing the candy on some part of it where it will be kept hot, but not cook. They must be slipped on to an oiled dish, and, needless to say, most carefully handled.

Other baskets are made with nougat, others with pastry, and the Swiss make what they call *Vacherin* with almond paste, and serve whipped cream in them; but the idea may be extended and improved upon by serving dried fruits or candies, or ice-cream in them, and they are a decided improvement on the paper baskets so often used for the last purpose, being eatable.

Swiss Vacherin.—Take half a pound of almond paste, three quarters of a pound of confectioners' sugar, and the white of one egg. Shave the almond paste, stir the egg and sugar together, and flavor with a little orange-flower water or wine; work all together with the hand into a smooth, stiff paste that will roll out; if there is a disposition to crack or crumble, use more white of egg and almond paste. Roll it just as you would pie crust on the pastry board, using

confectioners' sugar in place of flour. Line
small cups or tartlet moulds, or anything
that will make a good form for baskets,
which have been very slightly oiled. Put
them aside to harden and dry. Chop a
tablespoonful of blanched pistachio-nuts till
they are as fine as corn-meal, mix with an
equal quantity of granulated sugar. Trim
the edges of the cups or baskets with scissors, turn them out of the moulds, very carefully dip the edges in a saucer containing
white of egg beaten to liquid—the edges
only need to be just wet. Have the chopped
pistachio-nuts and sugar also in a saucer, dip
the wet edge of the cup lightly into it, and
shake gently. If properly done, the cups
will now have a pretty green border. When
these are filled with whipped cream, sweetened, flavored, and colored, they are called
Swiss Vacherin. Filled with plain whipped
cream, and the top covered with strawberries, they are called " Chantilly cups," but
they may be used in many decorative ways,

to hold preserves or candied fruits, etc., etc.

Little China Dishes.—This quaint recipe is from the immortal Mrs. Glasse, and on trial was found so unique and agreeable a variety to our modern fancies that with some little changes to suit our present ideas I give the last-century dainty. If you have any pretty-shaped little tin dishes, without fluting, to mould and bake them in, they are very little trouble to make. Take the yolks of two eggs, two small tablespoonfuls of sherry, and one of rose-water, beat together only enough to mix, then use as much fine flour as will make a firm paste that can be rolled out exceedingly thin. Cover some nicely shaped little tins slightly buttered,. press to the form, be careful the paste fits without creases, and bake in a cool oven. When the paste is crisp, with very little change of color, they are done. Do not touch them till they are cold, as they may be brittle. Stir the white of an egg with a

tablespoonful of rose-water and confectioners' sugar enough to make a smooth icing;
squeeze in the juice of half a lemon, and
when the little dishes are cold, ice the under
side only just thick enough to mask the
pastry; when they are dry and hard, turn
them over and ice the inside; do this with
great smoothness, to look as much like porcelain as possible.   If you choose, when the
icing is quite hard, you can wet the edge of
the dishes with white of egg and dip them
in chopped pistachio-nuts and sugar, like the
Chantilly baskets, or in nonpareils (the small-
est size).   They may be used to serve anything sweet, from jelly to candies.

Almond Trifles.—With the almond paste
used for Chantilly cups many trifles may
be made with very little trouble; for instance, mix a tablespoonful of flour with
the paste; roll it out; cut into circles; pinch
up two sides; place a little handle over the
centre, and in each open end, which must be
bent slightly upward, place a candied cherry.

Or cut a number of thin strips of paste, stick them together in the middle with white of egg, pass a strip of almond paste round so that the strips look like fagots of sticks, let them just color in the oven, sift sugar over them, and put them away. The paste may be rolled as thick as a pipe-stem and tied in knots, the surface just moistened, and sugar sifted over them; these also must only just take color in the oven. These are only suggestions for using up the trimmings from the cups.

XXXI.

Raspberry Charlotte Russe.—The simplest and quite the most effective way of making charlottes of any kind is the following : Take a strip of light cartridge or drawing paper from two to three inches wide, measure it round a mould the size you wish the charlotte to be, and cut it an inch larger; piece the two ends together, lapping an inch. Lay this paper circle on an ornamental dish (the one you wish to use), split lady-fingers, and stand them around it inside like a picket-fence, only as close together as they will go, inserting a pin from the outside through the paper and each cake as you do it. When you have lined the paper completely you will have a close frame of lady-fingers held in place by pins. Whip a pint of *perfectly sweet*

cream that is at least twenty-four hours old
and has been thoroughly chilled on ice.
Sweeten the cream with two tablespoonfuls
of powdered sugar, and flavor it with a tablespoonful of raspberry *juice* (not syrup) mixed
with a tablespoonful of powdered sugar;
sometimes the raspberry juice will color the
cream a beautiful faint pink, which cannot
be improved upon, but if it is not bright
enough in tint stir in one or two drops of
cochineal. If the weather is warm stand
the vessel containing the cream in ice; then
beat without stopping to skim the froth as
it rises. In about ten to fifteen minutes the
cream ought to be perfectly solid if all the
conditions were observed, and the beating
carried on in a cool, airy room. If, however, the cream is not solid enough to keep
shape, set it on ice for an hour and beat
again. Fill the centre of the frame of lady-
fingers, piling it high; decorate either with
chopped pistachio-nuts lightly sprinkled, or
with rings of angelica. The raspberry *juice*

used for flavoring is to be obtained at first-class druggists', where the best quality of soda-water is sold. It is unsweetened, and although I have kept it two or three months in cool weather, it often will not keep many weeks; it is therefore better to buy it by the gill or half-pint, if your druggist will sell it so, than to buy a large bottle, although it is so useful for making raspberry jelly, raspberry shrub, and many other things, that even a bottle is not likely to be wasted. It must not be confused with raspberry *syrup*, which is heavily sweetened, but not nearly so fragrant. Before serving the charlotte remove the pins and take the paper off.

Charlotte Russe with Gelatine.—Prepare a frame as in last recipe, also beat a pint of cream sweetened and flavored with wine or to taste; melt in a pint of milk half an ounce of gelatine. The French gelatine is very pure, easy to melt, and no more expensive than any other good kind, and for delicate uses preferable to them. Make the gelatine and milk into a custard with two eggs, sweeten with two tablespoonfuls of sugar, flavor to taste, and put to get cold, stirring it once in a while; when it begins to thicken round the sides of the vessel beat with the egg-beater till foamy. You have now a vessel of whipped custard and one of whipped cream, both cold; now mix the cream into the custard, a little at a time, giving the spoon a light upward movement; *do not stir it;* that deadens the cream; your object is to keep it light; when all is mixed, fill the frame of cake with the spongy mixture; decorate it either with drops and pipings of the mixture applied to the smooth surface, or with candied fruits cut into forms or various colored jellies.

Of course a charlotte russe can be varied in many ways. It may be filled with the custard made with chocolate, and so be brown charlotte, or the filling may have apricot or currant jelly whipped into it with the gelatine; this is an admirable change.

Almond Turban.—Make half a pound of fine puff-paste, give it nine turns, roll it the last time to the thickness of a dollar; have ready half a pound of almonds, blanched and chopped; put them in a bowl with half a pound of powdered sugar and the whites of two eggs, adding a very little more if the icing is too stiff to spread; spread the almond icing on the pastry as thick as a twenty-five-cent piece; with a sharp knife cut the pastry into strips two and a half inches long and one in breadth; bake these in a moderate oven a very pale brown; make a circle on a dish of some *firm* marmalade or jam; when the almond cakes are cold, dress them in a crown on the jam, which serves to keep them in place; fill the centre of the turban with vanilla ice-cream or simple whipped cream.

Fine Small Cakes for Dessert.—It may not be worth the while of a busy housekeeper within reach of a first-class confectioner's to make these, because, although when of fine quality they are always expensive, yet they are also tedious to make. Many, however, live in country towns, where there is no possibility of obtaining anything better than the sandy products of the country bakery.

A few really fine cakes can be made at a time, and kept in an air-tight box, with layers of paper between, for some time. In speaking, however, of the tediousness I would not discourage the reader, for there are few more tedious things in cooking than the rolling out, making, and baking of thin cookies or ginger-snaps, and the result attained so inadequate.

Rout Biscuits.—Boil a pound of sugar in half a pint of milk; grate into it the rind of a lemon when cold; rub half a pound of butter into a pound and a half of flour and a pound of almond paste grated fine; put as much carbonate of soda as would lie on a silver dime into the milk, and mix with the flour and almond paste; beat two eggs, and make the whole into a firm, smooth paste;

print this paste with very small butter moulds if you have them, making little cakes just like the tiny pats of butter one gets at city restaurants. Bake on a well-buttered pan in a quick oven a very pale yellow.

Macaroons.—These must be exempted from the charge of being tedious, they are so easily and quickly made. One pound of almond paste grated, one pound and a half of sugar, and the whites of seven eggs. Some confectioners use a teaspoonful of flour, with the idea that the macaroons are not so apt to fall. I recommend a trial of both methods; they will both be good. Stir the sugar and the beaten white of eggs together just enough to mix, then by degrees add the grated paste, mashing with the back of a fork till it forms a perfectly smooth paste. Oil several sheets of paper cut to the size of your baking-pans. Dripping-pans may be used if you have no regular baking-sheets. Lay a sheet of paper at the bottom of the pan. Put half a teaspoonful of the macaroon paste on a scrap of

buttered paper in the oven.   If it spreads
too much it requires a very little more sugar;
if it does not spread at all, or so little as to
leave the surface rough, it is too stiff, and
requires perhaps *half* the white of an egg, or
the finger dipped in water and laid on each
macaroon after they are on the paper is often
sufficient—a little practice is all that is necessary.   Lay the paste in half-teaspoonfuls
on the oiled or greased paper.   If the trial
one indicated that they were slightly too
stiff, lay a wet finger on each, sift powdered
sugar over, and then put a pinch of chopped
and blanched almonds in the centre with just
enough pressure to keep them in place.   As
the macaroon spreads in the oven the almonds scatter themselves.

Macaroons should be baked *about* twenty
minutes in a moderate oven.   They must be
taken out while they are a very pale brown,
but they must also be quite "set," or they
will fall.   If the oven is too quick they will
brown too soon; in that case leave the oven

door open, taking care that no cold draught can blow on the macaroons. You can tell if.they have browned too quickly by the cracks in them being still white and sticky. When done both the cracks and surface should be the same pale color. The maca-roons must be left five minutes in the pan after leaving the oven without being touched. At the end of that time they may be gently taken off the pans *on the papers*, from which they must not be detached until they are quite cold. Should they stick to the paper, moisten the back of it.

Fine Ginger Dessert Cakes.—Rub half a pound of fresh butter into three quarters of a pound of flour; beat three eggs with three quarters of a pound of powdered sugar and half a glass of rosewater, the grated peel of a lemon, and a teaspoonful of the best pow-dered ginger—use the ginger carefully, try-ing a level spoonful first. Then mix all into a paste. If the flavor of ginger is not strong enough, add more; they should taste well of

19

it, without being hot in the mouth. Roll the paste a quarter of an inch thick, and cut into small oval or round cakes, sift powdered sugar over them, and bake rather slowly a very pale brown.

XXXII

FINE CAKES AND SAUCES.

Madeleines.—Four ounces of butter, four ounces of the best flour, three ounces of sugar, a teaspoonful of orange-flower water, the yolks of four eggs, and rind of a lemon. Beat butter, sugar, and yolks of eggs together, then add the other ingredients; grate in the rind of half a lemon, and add the well-beaten whites of eggs last of all. Fill little moulds that have been buttered with washed butter, cover the tops with split almonds and sifted sugar; bake from thirty to forty minutes in a moderate oven. These cakes are sometimes served hot with apricot sauce.

Chestnut Croquettes.—Boil fifty sound chestnuts; take them out of the shells; reject all imperfect ones; keep the large pieces aside; pound the crumbs and most broken pieces

with an ounce of butter till very smooth;
then mix in a *small* cup of cream two ounces
of butter and one ounce of powdered sugar;
put the whole into a double boiler, and stir
in the beaten yolks of six eggs. Let the
mixture set. When cool, make it into balls;
in the centre of each ball put a piece of the
chestnut you have laid aside, dip the balls in
fine cracker meal and eggs, and fry a very
pale yellow. Serve with sifted sugar.

Very pretty cakes, very easily made, which
come under the French term *petits fours*, may
be given here.

Petits Fours.—Make rich cake mixture
thus: Wash three quarters of a pound of
butter to free it from excess of salt; squeeze
it dry in a cloth; beat it with the hand till
creamy; add three quarters of a pound of
powdered sugar; beat till light; then beat
in ten eggs, one by one, and sift in a pound
of dried and sifted flour. When all are well
beaten together, the paste or batter is ready
for use. Line some shallow pans (those used

for making rolled jelly-cake are best) with buttered paper; spread a layer of the mixture just as you would for jelly-cake, but much thicker, as when baked the sheets should not be more than the third of an inch thick. Bake slowly. When done, remove from the oven, but leave the cake undisturbed till cold. If the sheets are large, they may be cut exactly in half, spread thinly with some stiff marmalade or jelly; quince or apricot is best, but any rich flavor with some tartness will do; lay one half on the other, and press closely and very neatly together. Do each sheet of cake in the same way, varying the marmalade if you choose. Have ready a bowl of icing (either boiled French icing or what is called royal icing). Dust the top of the cakes with flour, which must be brushed off again, as it is only to absorb the grease. Flavor the icing with vanilla, and lay it on the centre of the cake; let it run over it, aiding with a knife dipped in water (shaking off the drops, however). The icing needs to be very neatly done, and must not be thicker than a twenty-five-cent piece. Now color the icing in the bowl pink, with a little cochineal, add a drop or two of extract of bitter almond or of lemon, either of which will agree with the vanilla that was in the white icing; then ice another sheet of cake in the same way; a third may be done with chocolate icing.

The beauty of these cakes will depend on the way they are cut. You may choose to make them tablets an inch wide and three inches long, or in lozenge shape—the true diamond—but in either case the cutting must be exact. The best way to have it so is to mark the lines very lightly with the point of a penknife on the icing, using a measure. Trim off the edge of the cake with a sharp knife, so that it is neat all round, no excess of marmalade oozing out, or tears of icing running down. Then warm a sharp carving-knife (I am supposing the cake is on a board), and cut through the lines you have marked, without hesitation, so that there may be no crumbs or roughness, which slow, over-careful cutting causes. When cut up you should have, if neatly done, an assortment of very delicious and ornamental cakes.

FRENCH SWEET SAUCES FOR PUDDINGS, ETC.

Sauce Madère à la Marmalade.—A half-pound of apricot marmalade; half a tumbler of Madeira or sherry; boil three minutes, then pass through a sieve, and serve as sauce to soufflées, cabinet puddings, etc.

Sauce des Œufs au Kirsch.—Beat the yolks of eight eggs, put them in a saucepan with half a tumbler of kirsch, five ounces of powdered sugar, and half the rind of a lemon grated. Stir all in a double boiler till the mixture sticks to the spoon; then remove from the boiling water; stir for a minute to prevent curdling; then it is ready to serve.

Chaudeau Sauce.—Take two whole eggs, six yolks of eggs, and eight lumps of sugar (each one rubbed on lemon-peel), two pints of Chablis, and the juice of half a lemon; beat them over a slow fire in a double boiler till a light froth is formed; be very careful the eggs do not curdle when the boiling-point is reached; take the sauce off the fire, and continue beating for a minute or two. If small streaks appear on the froth the sauce is done. Stir in a tablespoon-ful of fine rum, and the sauce is ready to serve.

Sherry Sauce for Puddings.—Six yolks of eggs, one ounce of sugar, half a pint of sher-ry, and the thin peel of a lemon. Beat the eggs with the sugar; when the wine is warm, stir them into it (let the lemon-peel steep in the wine while warming); stir all together till as thick as cream; then remove from the fire, and take out the peel. In making all these sauces with eggs the same precaution is required as in making custard.

Wine Sauce, No. 2.—Three gills of water, one cup of sugar, one teaspoonful of corn-starch, and one gill of wine. Mix the corn-starch with a little water; pour the rest boiling to it, stirring till smooth; then add the sugar, and boil for five minutes; then add the wine and a few drops of essence of lemon and the same of cinnamon. Use these flavorings drop by drop, as they differ in strength too much for an exact quantity to be given, and the taste must be the guide. Rum or brandy may be used instead of wine; then the cinnamon is omitted.

Apricot Sauces.—Half a small jar of apricot jam or marmalade; dissolve it in three quarters of a gill of water with the juice of a lemon; stir in three quarters of a gill of rum. This sauce is simply made hot, not boiled, and may be served cold with Baba or Savarin cake. Greengage marmalade may be substituted.

Whipped Sweet Sauce.—Put the yolks of four eggs into a double saucepan with two ounces of sugar, one glass of sherry, the juice of one lemon, and a speck of salt; beat all together; then set the saucepan over the fire, and whisk the sauce till it is a creamy froth, when it is ready to serve.

Very Fine Sweet Butter Sauce.—Wash four ounces of butter; squeeze it dry; beat it to a hard sauce with half a pound of powdered sugar; then put the yolks of two eggs in a cold bowl; stir it a minute, then add to it a little of the hard sauce; when well mixed add more, about a teaspoonful at a time; when the hard sauce is blended with the yolks of eggs, stir in by degrees a wineglass of brandy or rum. Keep on ice till wanted.

Vanilla Cream Sauce.—Put half a pint of fresh cream to boil, reserving a tablespoon-ful; mix this with a teaspoonful of flour; stir it into the cream, with a tablespoonful of sugar, when near boiling; when it boils, stir for five minutes or ten in a double boiler; then pour out the sauce, and stir in a small teaspoonful of vanilla and a few drops of ex-tract of rose or a teaspoonful of rose-water. Observe that the rose is used to give a dif-ferent tone to the vanilla, and not to impart its own flavor, therefore very little must be used.

Almond Sauce. — Dissolve four ounces of almond paste in half a pint of sweet cream by stirring in a double boiler (the almond paste should be grated first); when both are hot, add a tablespoonful of sugar and the yolk of an egg; stir till the egg thickens, then remove from the fire and serve.

XXXIII

SALADS AND CHEESE DISHES.

SALAD has come to form part of even the simplest dinners; and certainly cold meat and salad and excellent bread and butter make a meal by no means to be despised even by an epicure, while cold meat and bread and butter sound very untempting. The best dinner salad will perhaps always be white, crisp lettuce, with a simple French dressing, although, to those acquainted with it, escarole runs it hard, with its cool, watery ribs and crisp leaves. Elaborate salads, or those dressed with mayonnaise, are too heavy to form the latter part of an already sufficiently·nourishing meal, but for luncheons and suppers the rich salad is invaluable.

Salad which is to be eaten with game or to form a course at dinner may be a crisp white cabbage lettuce, water-cress, Romaine lettuce, or that most delicious form of endive, escarole.

The dressing should be the simple French dressing, about which so much has been written and said, and which is so easy that perhaps it is one reason why so few make it well. There is nothing to remember beyond the proportions, and so many keep the quantity of oil, vinegar, and pepper and salt in mind, but the manner of using them seems of no consequence ; but it is of so much consequence, if you do not want the vinegar on the leaves and the oil at the bottom of the salad bowl, that, well known as the formula is, I am going over it again with a few details that may help to fix the matter in mind.

In the first place it must be remembered that a wet leaf will repel oil, therefore the lettuce or other salad must be well dried before it is sent to table. This is best done by swinging it in a salad basket, and then spreading it between two cloths for a few minutes. Now it must be quite evident, if a leaf wet with water will refuse to retain oil, that one wet with vinegar will do the same; for this reason the leaves should be covered with oil *before* the vinegar is added, or the salad will be crude and very unlike what it should be if properly mixed in the following way:

Take lettuce as the example, although any of those mentioned are made in the same way. Have the lettuce dry in the salad bowl, put in the salad-spoon a saltspoonful of salt, a quarter one of pepper, and, holding it over the bowl, fill the spoon with oil; mix the salt and pepper well with it, and turn it over the salad; toss the salad lightly over and over till the leaves glisten, then add two (if for epicures, three or four) more spoonfuls of oil, then toss again over and over till every leaf is well coated with oil; then sprinkle in a saladspoonful of sharp vinegar. Toss again, and the salad is ready.

One salad less well known than it deserves to be is that made from the grape fruit. This is an especially grateful dish for spring breakfast, when cool, refreshing things are in order. Many tell me they have tried to eat grape fruit, but find it quite impossible on account of the intense bitter.

There is a very *slight* and pleasant bitter with grape fruit when properly prepared, but if by carelessness or ignorance even a small portion of the pith is left in it intense bitter is imparted to the whole.

Grape-fruit Salad. — Prepare the fruit, some hours before it is wanted, in the following way: Cut the fruit in four as you would an orange; separate the sections; then remove the pulp from each, taking care that no white pith or skin adheres to it. Put the pulp on the ice until just before serving; then dress with oil and vinegar exactly as directed for lettuce, etc.

Meat or fish salads should always be dressed with mayonnaise. I say nothing of the well-

known lobster and chicken salads, which are
so general that one is tempted to think the
majority of people do not know how excellent some other combination salads are.
Salmon salad—the fish flaked, laid on a bed
of crisp lettuce with a border of the leaves,
and masked with mayonnaise, with a garnish of aspic—is both handsome and delicious; but cold halibut, or even cod—any
firm fish that flakes, in fact—make delightful salads, and acceptable to many who cannot eat lobster.   In the way of meat salads,
partridge or grouse are far daintier than
chicken, prepared in just the same way.
There is one point, however, which should
be observed in making all meat salads: it is
that the material should be well dressed with
oil, vinegar, and condiments before the mayonnaise is put on.   Usually one of two courses
is followed: either the meat is left dry, the
mayonnaise being supposed sufficient, or it is
dressed with mayonnaise and then masked
with it.   In the latter case the salad is far

too rich; in the former it is flat, because mayonnaise, if rightly made, has not acidity enough to flavor the meat; therefore it and the celery or other salad mixed with it should be bathed with French dressing before it is masked.

With these general rules any salad may be made; but as variety is the spice of the table, it may be borne in mind that in spring a sprig of mint, very finely chopped, gives a fragrance to lettuce, as does chervil or borage, parsley, or a tiny bit of onion. To a game salad nothing should be added.

No recipe is needed for mayonnaise, it having been given in the chapter on cold sauces.

In the course of these chapters several cheese dishes have been given, but there are a few others especially appropriate to the cheese and salad course, where it constitutes part of the dinner, which I will include. Cheese dishes are far less popular in this country than in Europe, but there are families whose masculine members eat no sweets,

20

and for whom a dainty cheese dish would be very acceptable.

Genoa Ramaquin.—Cut a slice of Vienna or other baker's bread, half an inch thick, lengthwise of the loaf, so that it covers the bottom of a fire-proof dish—a soufflé pan well buttered is excellent; beat two eggs and half a pint of milk together; add a level saltspoonful of salt; pour this custard over the bread, and leave it an hour to soak. Pour off any custard that may not be absorbed; dust the bread with pepper; then cover with the following mixture: dissolve as much rich cheese shaved in half a gill of cream as will cover the bread an inch thick, stirring it over a slow fire. Season with pepper and salt, and pour the cheese over the bread. Put it in the oven, and bake for half an hour, or till quite brown.

Cheese Puffs.—Line patty-pans with puff-paste, and fill three parts full with the following mixture: put a gill of cream in a double boiler with two ounces of grated

cheese (half Parmesan if liked), a saltspoonful of salt, a pinch of pepper, a pinch of
sugar, and a large teaspoonful of butter;
when all is melted to a thick custard, break
into it two eggs well whipped. The mixture is only to be made hot enough to melt
the cheese, not to boil.

Cheese Sticks.—Take a piece of light bread
dough about the size of a teacup, roll it out
on a pastry-board, spread it with bits of firm
butter, dredge with flour, fold and roll, repeat until you have rolled in two ounces of
butter, just as for puff-paste; now roll the
pastry out the third of an inch thick, cut
into strips half an inch wide and any length
you think proper, lay them very straight on
a baking-sheet, and bake slowly a *very* light
brown; remove from the oven, let them cool,
then brush them over with white of egg, and
roll them thickly in grated Parmesan; return
for a minute or two to the oven. These are
very good with salad, but cannot easily be
made in warm weather. Should the pastry

get too soft while rolling, put it on ice, and it is better to do so at all times before cutting into strips, so that the "sticks" may be quite straight.

INDEX.

THE END.

MISS CORSON'S FAMILY LIVING ON $500 A YEAR.

Family Living on $500 a Year. A Daily Reference Book for Young and Inexperienced Housewives. By JULIET CORSON. 16mo, Cloth, $1 25.

If we ever get as much as $500 a year we shall purchase this book and live like a prince. . . . It goes carefully through the expenses of daily living, and indicates the thousand and one ways in which a penny can be saved and another penny put where it will do most good. A book of this kind placed in the hands of those who have very limited means will show that they can live very comfortably and have quite enough to eat on a very small sum.—*N. Y. Herald.*

It is a helpful working book, sensible and practical, and tells how to buy, cook, and serve all sorts of food; how to can, pickle, and preserve; and how to arrange and serve luncheons, dinners, and teas, all in the most economical manner consistent with appetizing results.—*Sunday-School Times,* Philadelphia.

Food-economist, cook-book, and instructor in table service all in one. . . . The book is a capital one, and every housekeeper should feel grateful to the able and painstaking author.—*N. Y. Post.*

The production of a lady who understands her subject thoroughly, and who earnestly wishes to help others towards the same useful knowledge. . . . A book of this sort (and Miss Corson is the best able to produce it of any one we know) is a great aid, and the more it is circulated the more households will be made happy.—*Churchman, N. Y.*

Every house-keeper, whether coming within the scope of the author's effort or not, will find many instructive hints, a due regard for which will be conducive to the improved physical well-being and increased mental serenity of the various members of her household.—*St. Louis Republican.*

PUBLISHED BY HARPER & BROTHERS, NEW YORK.

☞ HARPER & BROTHERS *will send the above work by mail, postage prepaid, to any part of the United States or Canada, on receipt of the price.*

MRS. SHERWOOD'S MANNERS AND SOCIAL USAGES IN AMERICA.

Manners and Social Usages in America. A Book of Etiquette. By Mrs. John Sherwood. pp. 448. New and Enlarged Edition, Revised by the Author. 16mo, Extra Cloth, $1 25.

Mrs. Sherwood's admirable little volume differs from ordinary works on the subject of etiquette, chiefly in the two facts that it is founded on its author's personal familiarity with the usages of really good society, and that it is inspired by good-sense and a helpful spirit. . . . We think Mrs. Sherwood's little book the very best and most sensible one of its kind that we ever saw.—*N. Y. Commercial Advertiser.*

We have no hesitation in declaring it to be the best work of the kind yet published. The author shows a just appreciation of what is good-breeding and what is snobbishness. . . . In happy discriminations the excellence of Mrs. Sherwood's book is conspicuous.—*Brooklyn Union.*

It is a sensible and pleasantly written volume, which has already won recognition as one of the best books of its kind, and this new edition is called for by the heartiness with which the public has endorsed the work.—*Courier*, Boston.

A sensible, comprehensive book, which has endured criticism successfully, and deserves now to be regarded the best book of its kind published in this country. . . . A better guide than Mrs. Sherwood's book through the paths of social usages we do not know. The book is a handsome one, as it ought to be.—*Christian Intelligencer*, N. Y.

Published by HARPER & BROTHERS, New York.

☞ Harper & Brothers *will send the above work by mail, postage prepaid, to any part of the United States or Canada, on receipt of the price.*

BOOKS FOR THE HOUSEHOLD.

MRS. HENDERSON'S PRACTICAL COOKING.
Practical Cooking and Dinner Giving. A Treatise containing Practical Instructions in Cooking; in the Combination and Serving of Dishes, and in the Fashionable modes of Entertaining at Breakfast, Lunch, and Dinner. By MARY F. HENDERSON. Illustrated. 12mo, Water-proof Cover, $1 50.

MRS. HENDERSON'S DIET FOR THE SICK.
Diet for the Sick. A Treatise on the Values of Foods, their Application to Special Conditions of Health and Disease, and on the Best Methods of their Preparation. By MARY F. HENDERSON. Illustrated. 12mo, Cloth, $1 50

MRS. WASHINGTON'S UNRIVALLED COOKBOOK. The Unrivalled Cook-Book and Housekeeper's Guide. By Mrs. WASHINGTON. 12mo, Water-proof Cover, $2 00.

MRS. SMITH'S VIRGINIA COOKERY - BOOK.
Virginia Cookery - Book. By MARY STUART SMITH. 12mo, Cloth, $1 50; 4to, Paper, 25 cents.

BAZAR COOKING RECEIPTS. Cooking Receipts from *Harper's Bazar*. 32mo, Paper, 25 cents; Cloth, 40 cents.

MISS OAKEY'S BEAUTY IN DRESS. Beauty in Dress. By MISS OAKEY. 16mo, Cloth, $1 00.

MRS. DEWING'S (MISS OAKEY) BEAUTY IN THE HOUSEHOLD. Beauty in the Household. By Mrs. T. W. DEWING, Author of "Beauty in Dress." Illustrated. 16mo, Cloth, $1 00.

COAN'S OUNCES OF PREVENTION. Ounces of Prevention. By TITUS MUNSON COAN, M.D. 12mo, Paper, 25 cents; Cloth, 50 cents.

MRS. CHURCH'S MONEY-MAKING FOR LADIES. Money-Making for Ladies. By ELLA RODMAN CHURCH. 16mo, Cloth, 90 cents.

WALKER'S HINTS TO WOMEN ON THE CARE OF PROPERTY. Hints to Women on the Care of Property. By ALFRED WALKER. 32mo, Paper, 20 cents; Cloth, 35 cents.

MISS CORSON'S FAMILY LIVING. Family Living on $500 a Year. A Daily Reference Book for Young and Inexperienced Housewives. By JULIET CORSON. 16mo, Cloth, $1 25.

MRS. HERRICK'S HOUSE-KEEPING MADE EASY. House-keeping Made Easy. By CHRISTINE TERHUNE HERRICK. 16mo, Cloth, $1 00.

PUBLISHED BY HARPER & BROTHERS, NEW YORK.

☞ HARPER & BROTHERS *will send any of the above works, postage prepaid, to any part of the United States or Canada, on receipt of the price.*